THE OTHER FELIX

Keir Graff

THE OTHER FELIX

ROARING BROOK PRESS
NEW YORK

Text copyright © 2011 by Keir Graff

Illustrations copyright © 2011 Oriol Vidal

Published by Roaring Brook Press

Roaring Brook Press is a division of Holtzbrinck Publishing Holdings
Limited Partnership

175 Fifth Avenue, New York, New York 10010

mackids.com

Library of Congress Cataloging-in-Publication Data

Graff, Keir, 1969–
    The other Felix / Keir Graff. — 1st ed.
       p.   cm.
    Summary: Worrying about his father losing his job and the bully at
school, fourth-grader Felix has terrifying dreams of the same monster-
filled place every night until he meets someone there who looks and
sounds strangely familiar.
    ISBN: 978-1-59643-655-8
    [1. Nightmares—Fiction.   2. Bullies—Fiction.   3. Schools—
Fiction.   4. Family problems—Fiction.   5. Fear—Fiction.]   I. Title.

PZ7.G751575Oth 2011
[Fic]—dc22

                                                            2010050605

Roaring Brook Press books are available for special promotions and
premiums. For details contact: Director of Special Markets,
Holtzbrinck Publishers.

First edition 2011
Book design by Jay Colvin
Printed in September 2011 in the United States of America by
RR Donnelley & Sons Company, Harrisonburg, Virginia

1   3   5   7   9   10   8   6   4   2

For the real Felix

ONE

Felix woke up in the woods, wearing his pajamas. He looked around for his slippers, but his slippers were under his bed, and he wasn't lying in his bed. He was lying on dry, rust-colored pine needles. The bed of needles was soft until he rolled over. Then the needles turned sharp and pricked him.

He stood up. There were tall, thin trees all around him, their bare trunks marching off into gray mist. High above, their green branches touched, forming a ceiling. Nothing moved in the trees, not a bird, not a bug. He listened, but the woods were completely silent except for the sound of his own breathing.

Felix shivered in his thin pajamas.

"Well," he said. "There's nothing here, so I may as well see what's over there."

He started walking. He wondered what time it was. In the dim light it was hard to tell. The ground rose under his feet. He was going uphill. The dirt he walked on was worn into a path. But the trees were growing closer together, and it was getting darker.

Up ahead he saw a flight of stone steps climbing the hill. The stones were old and crumbled and had moss growing in the cracks between them.

He climbed the steps, counting as he went. ". . . thirty-six, thirty-seven, thirty-eight, thirty-nine."

Then he stood at the top. He had expected to find something, maybe a house, because surely steps were made to lead somewhere. But there was nothing, only the woods crowding the daylight from the sky. On the other side of the steps, the path ran downhill.

"Well," he said. "I guess I'll keep going and see what's at the end of the path."

But his feet didn't move. Maybe they weren't listening. The way ahead did look awfully dark.

Then Felix heard something. Somewhere in the forest, a moan rose and fell and then trailed away.

Felix listened, but the woods were silent again. Maybe it had only been wind blowing through the pine boughs. Once again he got ready to follow the path downhill.

Then a branch broke with a crack.

"Hello?" called Felix. "Hello?"

He heard the clatter of hooves on rock. He heard wet, ragged breaths. He glimpsed something, fast as quicksilver—curly horns, scaly hide, spiky tail—and then it was gone again.

It was nothing he'd ever seen in a zoo. But he had seen something like it somewhere. As he remembered, his heart started beating more quickly.

He had seen it in a book about monsters.

Felix spun around. It was behind him. No, it was in front of him. He couldn't tell. He held his breath, listening.

It grew very quiet, as if the monster were listening for Felix, too.

Then Felix heard snuffling sounds. The monster was trying to catch his scent.

There was a shuddering inhalation, a low growl, and then the monster started coming toward him, much faster than before. Rocks slid and scattered as its hooves kicked the earth. Its breath huffed and chuffed, its belly making hungry rumbling sounds.

Felix turned and ran back down the hill. He watched his feet flying down the broken steps as if they belonged to someone else. He made it to the bottom of the steps without falling, but as he stepped onto the path, his ankle twisted and he stumbled and fell.

Sprawled on the ground, he looked back, up the stone staircase, expecting to see the monster galloping down. But he saw nothing. The monster was still hidden in the trees.

Felix stood up and started running again. The sharp pine needles hurt his bare feet. His throat burned as he sucked air into his lungs. He felt as if he were running in slow motion. Surely the monster could run faster than him.

The monster was louder now, crazed with hunger. It sounded like a garbage truck crashing through the woods. Any minute now, it would come into the open.

He ran harder. The monster was still loud, but it wasn't getting any louder. Maybe Felix could get away.

He saw the clearing, the bed of pine needles where he first woke up. He thought for a moment that he was safe. Then he realized that he wasn't safe at all. He was in a huge forest far away from his home. In a moment, the monster would storm into the clearing. Felix would have to keep running, into the dark trees on the other side.

As he crossed the deep bed of pine needles, his

feet dropped out from under him. He fell, through the forest floor, into darkness—

—and into his own bed.

He was awake. His heart was racing and he was breathing hard. The sweaty sheets were tangled around his feet. He was still scared—he felt as though he were in two places at once and, at any moment, his bedroom might turn into a forest filled with monsters.

But the city's light glimmered around the corners of his window shades. Far below, a car horn honked. Two sirens wailed in a sad duet. And the walls of his dark room stayed white.

Felix looked at the glowing numbers on his clock. It was three in the morning. He pulled up his blankets and reached for his stuffed aardvark. He was too old for stuffed animals, he knew, but a boy who was chased by monsters needed a friend.

Soon his heart had slowed to a normal bump-bump, bump-bump. His breathing became deep and even. And in a little while he fell asleep again.

TWO

Felix Schwartzwalder was an ordinary boy with orange hair who lived in a tall building in a big city. He had lived in the city all his life and had never left it. While he had seen pictures of forests, rivers, and mountains in books, he had never seen a forest, a river, or a mountain in real life.

What he saw, from his bedroom window on the fortieth floor, were streets that ran to all points of the compass and kept running out of sight. The streets were lined with buildings, most of them smaller than his own. But, in the distance, he could see tall skyscrapers crowded together, their spires so high they were sometimes lost in the clouds. The skyscrapers were like a forest made of metal and glass.

The streets below crossed each other at right angles, cutting the city into blocks. Most of these blocks were hard and bright with concrete, but some of them were green and furred with trees. And some of these green blocks had no buildings on them at all. These were the city parks.

Felix loved going to the parks. When he played, three trees became a forest, a puddle became an ocean, and a rock became a mountain. He didn't always play explorer. Sometimes he liked nothing better than to sit on a shaded bench and read his books. He liked the sigh of the wind through the whispering leaves and the chatter of the little hopping birds that begged for crumbs.

But Felix didn't go to the park very often. His parents worked hard and they didn't have much time for playing. Felix would have liked to go to the park with some of the kids from school, but his parents had a rule that they had to meet the other kids' parents before he could play with them. And his parents never had time to meet other parents because they were always working.

Actually, Felix wasn't entirely sure that he had any friends—real friends, that is.

Felix's mother worked in a hospital. Felix had been allowed to go with her one day to see the big, round desk she shared with two other mothers. The desk was in the middle of a large room filled with toys for the kids and chairs for their parents. The walls were painted with rainbow roads, cloud castles, and dancing animals. Felix thought that it must be nice to work in a place where so many kids played happily. But his mother, whose pretty brown hair was threaded with silver, seemed tired after work. She asked him questions about his day and murmured, "Really?" and "Is that so?" while he answered. Sometimes she asked him the same question twice.

Felix's father was often away, working long hours on something he called "the Project." Felix did not know what the Project was, but his parents talked about it often. Felix's father was a tall man who chuckled a lot and had a funny, lopsided smile. But he didn't laugh as much when he thought Felix wasn't listening. Many of his sentences started with the words, "I'm worried about . . ." If the Project did not go better soon, his father had told his mother, it would be very bad for all of them.

Felix went to school in a very old building across the street from the very new building in which he lived. This year, in the fourth grade, his desk was next to an empty desk by the window. The view from his classroom window was very different from the view from his bedroom window. When his teacher, Miss Olu, said "Pencils down," he liked to look out at the old trees swaying in the wind. There were so many things in motion and they never seemed to move the same way twice.

He liked his teacher and his classmates. He was pretty good at reading and math, but he was pretty great at drawing. Unfortunately, Miss Olu did not give grades for drawing, and art class was only once a week.

Every day at three o'clock, the crossing guard stopped both lanes of traffic while he walked across the busy street. Then he went back into his building. After saying hello to the doorman, he rode the elevator to the thirty-ninth floor and knocked on the door of the apartment directly below the one in which he lived. This was the home of Mrs. Nowak, his babysitter.

"Who is it?" Mrs. Nowak would call, even though he was the only boy she babysat, and even though he had never seen anyone else visit her.

"It's Felix, Mrs. Nowak," he would answer. Maybe she expected that, one day, another boy would show up in his place.

After she said "Come in," he would open the door, take off his backpack and his coat, and hang them on the doorknob. She always reminded him to shut the door, even though he never forgot to do it.

9

Mrs. Nowak's apartment smelled like hot apple cider, but not because she had a pan on the stove. She had air fresheners plugged into the electrical outlets that made the scent both night and day. Felix thought it smelled like Halloween.

His babysitter was old and did not have any kids of her own. She liked to watch TV and had many rules that Felix had to follow. He was not allowed to get his own snack and he was not allowed to watch TV. He was not allowed to have more than three toys with him in her home. He was not allowed to run or yell. All that was left, besides sitting quietly, was doing homework or reading.

Mostly, he read Mrs. Nowak's books, many of which had belonged to her husband. Mr. Nowak had been dead for a long time. His books were about far-off and long-ago places and the people who explored them. There were high mountains where the climbers grew beards of ice. There were jungles where spiders as big as hubcaps lived in ruined temples hidden by vines. There were ships wrecked on rocky islands. And when Felix grew tired of reading he sat and looked out the window, waiting for his mother to knock on Mrs. Nowak's door and take him home.

Sometimes as early as five thirty, but never later

than six fifteen, Felix's mother would knock on Mrs. Nowak's door.

"Who is it?" Mrs. Nowak would ask.

She did, however, trust Felix's mother to shut the door without being reminded. If it was Friday, Felix's mother would give Mrs. Nowak some money. Then Felix and his mother would walk down the hall, ride the elevator up one floor, and walk down the hall to their own door.

After dinner, if Felix had any homework, they worked on it together. If he didn't have any homework, they watched TV together. Felix's mother sometimes fell asleep on the couch. As she leaned against him, her head would suddenly become very heavy on the top of his head. When this happened, he didn't wake her, just listened to her slow, deep breathing. When she woke up, she always pretended that she hadn't fallen asleep.

"Goodness," she would say, "look at the time."

They read books together at bedtime. Felix would read one chapter aloud and then, while he lay back on his pillow and looked at the green star stickers on his ceiling, his mother would read one. Sometimes, Felix's father would come home before his mother turned out the lights.

"How was work, Dad?" Felix would ask.

"Another day, another dime," his father would say, messing up Felix's hair.

If he got home early enough, and he wasn't too tired, Felix's father would take off his tie and sit on Felix's bed to read a chapter. Though Felix thought that his mother was a much better reader, he always listened politely to his father. Sometimes his father's breath was stale, which made Felix wrinkle his nose. And when his father kissed Felix's cheek, whiskers scratched his face.

But he didn't really mind anything that happened while he was awake. Because when he was asleep, he had bad dreams.

THREE

He woke up in the pine needles again. The light was still gray and the air was still chilly. But this time he wasn't cold. He had gone to sleep wearing his robe and slippers and he was still wearing them in his dream. He was proud of himself for planning ahead.

He stood up, brushing pine needles off his robe and shaking them out of the pockets. The woods looked exactly the same as before. And they were just as silent as before, too.

He remembered that he hadn't heard the monster until he followed the path. So he didn't want to go looking for trouble.

"I'll just stay right here until this dream is over," he said.

He stood there, waiting to wake up.

After a while his legs got tired, so he sat down. After he had sat for a while, he started to get cold, despite his robe and slippers.

"Well," he said, "if I'm walking, at least I'll be warm."

He decided to go in the opposite direction, away from the stone steps. Maybe the path beyond the steps led to a ruined temple where the monster lived. So he turned and walked the other way. Swinging his arms to keep warm, he walked slowly, still watching and listening carefully.

After a little while, the ground began to slope downhill and the trees grew closer together. He picked his way through them cautiously, his ears pricked for danger.

A thicket of thornbushes blocked his path. Their branches were thick and oily, coiled like razor wire, with thorns as long as his little finger. He changed direction, but the thornbushes suddenly seemed to be everywhere. He changed direction again, but the bushes grew even thicker. And their thorns were even longer.

He turned and turned again, but it was hopeless. The evil thornbushes blocked his path. There was nowhere to go but back.

By the time he got to the clearing, he was tired and hungry. He wished he'd thought to put a candy bar in his pocket before going to bed. But he was so tired that he thought he would be able to sleep, even despite the cold. He lay down in the pine needles and closed his eyes.

Then he heard it. A deep, echoing *howf!* The sound of the monster clearing its throat. It seemed to come from nowhere and everywhere at once. But it might have been coming from the thornbushes.

Felix climbed to his feet and ran off toward the stone steps. It seemed better than sitting and waiting for the monster to come and catch him.

Everything in the forest looked so alike that he wasn't at all sure he was going the right way. But then the ground sloped upward. And the trees crowded around the path. And he saw the steps.

He stopped and listened. He didn't hear anything. He held his breath. But he still couldn't hear anything except the beating of his own heart.

He climbed the steps. At the top, once again, his feet didn't want to move. But this time, he willed them forward.

The path went downhill, through trees crowded so close on either side that it felt as though he were walking down a hallway. Then the path climbed out of the trees and wound through a field of boulders. Some of the boulders were the size of cars, and some were even as big as houses.

Above the trees, the sky was lighter, but still the sun didn't shine.

The path came to a sheer cliff, tall as a building. The path turned and followed the cliff wall. A steep, forested hill rose up on the other side. Suddenly, the ground fell away to a deep valley choked with trees. Felix saw a dull gleam of water and, rising up from the trees, a wooden tower.

He didn't have time to think about the tower. Blocking the trail ahead of him was a monster.

Big as a street sweeper, it had a matted coat snagged with thorns and pine needles. Its antlers were sharp and terrible. The scales on its haunches were rough like stone and its hooves were black and shiny. Its front legs ended in sharp claws that raked the ground. The monster's massive head was lowered as if it was gathering itself to spring. Its ruby eyes, deep in their sockets, gleamed with animal cunning.

Felix screamed.

And then he ran.

He ran back to the cliff wall, rounded a boulder, and looked frantically for a hiding place. Behind him, the monster let out a bellow that boomed and echoed in the silence. Its hooves thundered down the trail.

Felix found what he was looking for, a narrow passage between two massive boulders, big enough for a boy but too small for a monster the size of a street sweeper. He slipped inside, ran—and stopped. The passageway ended abruptly. He turned around, wondering how long the monster's front legs were.

There was a loud clatter of hooves and a shadow flew by the opening between the boulders. Felix's heart rose. The monster had run right by him.

Then the clatter stopped and Felix's heart sank. The monster picked its way carefully back up the trail. Its huge head appeared in the opening, blocking all the light.

Felix turned and looked at the rock blocking his escape. He stood on tiptoe and stretched his arms but he wasn't tall enough to reach the top. He jumped up. His fingertips just went over.

He took three steps back toward the monster, getting so close he could feel hot breath on his neck. Then he ran and jumped, reaching up with both hands. The top of the rock was smooth and it was hard to hold on. His hands slipped backward. He kicked furiously, searching for a toehold. Then he heard a roar and felt a tug on his bathrobe.

His toe found a bump. His fingers found a crack.

Arms trembling, he pulled himself up out of the narrow passageway. He turned and looked down. The monster's front leg searched furiously, a tatter of green flannel bathrobe fluttering from its claws.

Felix saw now that he could climb from one rock to another and then to the top of a house-sized rock. He went quickly, feeling certain that the monster, with its hooves and claws, was not a rock climber.

At the top he stopped, panting. He had lost his right slipper, but at the moment he wasn't worried about that. He circled the top of the rock, peering over the sides. It was like being on the roof of a two-story house. He was pretty certain he was safe. Of course, he didn't know how high a street-sweeper-sized monster could jump.

The monster grunted and groaned. Rocks slid and crashed as it tried desperately to reach Felix. Then the monster roared again, as loud as a subway train going around a curve. The roar boomed off the cliff face, down the hillside, and into the neighboring valley, the echoes answering each other as they faded away.

The monster turned and began walking away. Felix breathed a sigh of relief. He smiled.

Then the monster turned around.

Felix's smile froze.

The monster pawed the ground. It lowered its massive head and charged, galloping faster and faster until it smashed into the house-sized rock. The rock lurched backward, and Felix slipped and fell.

FOUR

"What happened last night?" Felix's mother asked him in the morning. She was yawning and her words sounded stretched out.

"I had a bad dream," Felix told her.

Felix's mother's yawn turned into a laugh. "It must have been a really bad dream if you tore your bathrobe and ate your slipper."

Felix, standing sleepily by his bed, didn't think that was very funny.

"A monster tore my bathrobe with its claw," he said. "I lost the slipper when I was trying to get away."

Felix's mother got down on her stomach on the floor and looked under the bed, pulling toys out o the way with her long arms. Then she took all the blankets off the bed and shook them out. She frowned.

"You shouldn't sleep in your slippers," she said. "Oh well, it will turn up. I can get your robe mended at the cleaner's."

Felix's mother made toasted raisin bagels for breakfast. Her own bagel grew cold on the counter while she hurried around, getting ready for the day. Felix's father was already gone. Felix chewed his bagel quietly. He was worried about going to bed that night. He didn't want to see any monsters. He decided to stay awake all night so he wouldn't dream.

Felix's mother came into the kitchen and took a big drink of coffee. "Hurry up, Felix," she said, and took another drink. "It's time to go to school."

At school, there was a new boy sitting next to Felix at the desk by the window. The new boy was big, with curly, sandy-brown hair and a freckled nose. Felix had liked the view before. But now there was a big boy sitting in the desk by the window, and the big boy blocked the view.

"Children," said Miss Olu, "this is Chase. Chase is new to this school and new to this city, too. I am sure you will make Chase feel welcome in our school and in our city. Welcome, Chase."

The kids said hi to Chase, their voices all crowded together. The new kid held his head high and looked people in the eye. But he didn't answer their friendly greetings with even a little smile.

Outside, past Chase's big head, Felix could see the green leaves on the trees turning yellow.

After lunch, after recess, came math class. Felix didn't mind math class. He enjoyed making numbers and the symbols for addition, subtraction, multiplication, and division. He liked the idea that marks on paper could stand in for things in the real world. But sometimes he got so interested in the shapes of numbers that he forgot he was supposed to be finding a solution.

That day, Miss Olu had a surprise: new calculators. She walked through the classroom, leaving one black-and-silver calculator on each desk. The kids started pushing buttons right away. Jasper Jones said that the calculators were boring; the screens weren't even in color. Marina Weir showed everyone how the calculator would turn off when she held her thumb over the solar panel.

Miss Olu returned to the front of the room and told them to be quiet. Then she explained the lesson, which was about dividing numbers where there was a remainder. Felix pressed the buttons. It was easy enough, but it wasn't as much fun as drawing the numbers.

After math came something better: art class. Today they would have free drawing. Miss Olu asked the students to return their calculators to the materials cabinet and to take one set of colored pencils for each pair of desks.

"I'll do it," said Chase. He carried the calculators away and returned with the pencils. But before he had even set them down, Chase started grabbing all the good colors: red, orange, blue, black, and gray. He was too fast for Felix.

Felix was left with yellow, purple, tan, brown, and green. At least he liked green.

He had an idea. He would draw a map of the land where he went in his dreams. He would draw the forest in green, the path in tan, and the thorn-bushes in brown. He looked longingly at the gray and black pencils. But the monsters would have to be purple and yellow.

"What are you looking at?" said Chase.

"Nothing," said Felix.

"Look at your own drawing," said Chase.

Chase was drawing a race car that looked like a spaceship, or maybe it was a spaceship that looked like a race car.

Felix started drawing. He drew the clearing

with the pine needles and the trees and the thorn-bushes. He drew the path and the stone stairway. Working quickly, he drew the rocky place and the cliff and the valley. He had never had dreams, good or bad, that he remembered so well when he was awake. If he had the blue pencil he might have drawn the water he had glimpsed, but he didn't know whether it was a river or a lake anyway. He made a square wooden tower, coloring it brown. Then he started in on the monsters. He pressed hard, using lots of color, making squiggles for the parts he didn't know how to draw.

His heart beat faster. He wondered how hard it would be to stay awake that night.

Suddenly, he heard laughter.

"What is *that*?" asked Chase.

"The Dream Land of Monsters," said Felix.

"And what are those blobby things?" asked Chase.

"Monsters," said Felix.

"Monsters! Those are monsters? They don't even look real. I'm drawing race cars and rockets and robots," said Chase. "And sharks and cheetahs. Monsters are stupid."

Felix turned the other way and hid his drawing with his arm.

At the end of art class, Miss Olu told the students

to put the pencils back in the materials cabinet. "I'll do it," said Chase.

Felix put his pencils in the box. Chase took the box to the cabinet, standing last in line. Miss Olu was finding her place in her book and wasn't paying attention.

Felix kept watching Chase. Chase put the pencils in the cabinet. Then he walked over to the coat hooks at the back of the room. He took a black-and-silver calculator out of his pocket and put it in his backpack.

Felix turned around quickly. He raised his hand to tell Miss Olu what he had seen. But her eyes were on the page. He waved his hand a little bit but she still didn't look up.

"Miss Olu?" he said nervously. His own voice sounded strange to him, high and shy, like a little kid's.

Miss Olu looked up. "Yes, Felix?"

Then Chase sat down beside him.

Felix put his hand down. "Um, nothing," he said. "I forgot what I was going to say."

Some of the kids laughed, but Felix stayed silent.

That night, Felix's father came home in time for dinner.

"How was your day, Dad?" asked Felix.

"Another day, another nickel," said his father.

"That bad, huh?" asked his mother.

"Oh, it's fine," said his father. "We'll be fine."

"Will I still be able to get allowance?" asked Felix.

"Even if I get paid in nickels, you'll still get allowance," said his father, grinning. "But you might have to take a pay cut, too."

"Really?" asked Felix.

"Your father is only kidding," said his mother.

After dinner, Felix's father helped him with his math. Miss Olu had told them to check their work with a calculator. Felix's father's calculator was bigger than the ones at school and had all sorts of strange mathematical symbols on it. While he hunted for the plus and minus buttons, he thought of the school calculator at the bottom of Chase's backpack. He both wished he had said something to Miss Olu and was glad he hadn't.

After homework, his father listened while Felix read a chapter from his book. Felix's mother always corrected him if he said something wrong or skipped some words by mistake. But Felix's father rarely interrupted.

When Felix was done with the chapter he put the book into his father's hands.

"Now you read," he said.

"But you're such a good reader, Felix."

Felix just shook his head. He liked listening better. It was easier to imagine the story that way.

Afterward, when Felix's father turned out the light and tucked him in, Felix took a deep breath.

"Dad," he said, "I'm afraid to go to sleep."

His father sighed. "Why's that, Felix?"

"Monsters," he said.

"You have dreams about monsters?"

"I think they're nightmares."

Felix's father patted his chest. "We all have bad dreams sometimes. But not every night."

"I have them every night," said Felix.

"Well, you'll have to try to think of something else. If you think about monsters all day, it's only natural that you'll dream about them at night."

"I don't think about monsters all day. I don't even like monsters."

"Well, how do you think the monsters get in your head?"

"I don't know."

Felix's father thought for a moment. Then he said: "Well, you need to chase those monsters out with good thoughts. Think about something that makes you happy."

Felix thought hard. Going to the zoo made him

happy, especially when his parents bought him popcorn. But he didn't see how thinking about the zoo would scare away monsters.

"Got it?" asked his father. "What are you thinking of?"

"It's a secret," said Felix.

"Like a birthday wish?"

Felix nodded.

"Good night," said his father. "And good luck."

His father kissed him on the top of his head and went out into the hall. When the door swung open, the hall light was bright like a searchlight. Then the door swung shut and it went out.

Felix burrowed down into the blankets. He grabbed his aardvark and squeezed it until he thought the stuffing would burst out of it. He forced his eyes to open wide. After a while, he could see everything in his room even though it was dark: his beanbag chair, his dresser, his toy chest, his bookshelf, and the pile of dirty laundry spilling out from behind the door.

"Stay awake," he whispered. "Stay awake, Felix!"

He was afraid to fall asleep. But he was also tired. Very, very tired.

FIVE

Felix's head hurt. He was lying on his back. Rocks rose up all around him. It was as though he'd fallen into a hole. He couldn't see the monster. Slowly, he realized that the monster was on the other side of the biggest rock, the one that he'd fallen off. He was safe for the moment.

The monster bellowed and stamped its feet. Then it thundered down the path again. There was a dull thud as it butted the boulder and then a grinding sound as the boulder began to tip over. The boulder's shadow fell over Felix and he turned and looked for a way out. In a shadow, he saw a glimmer of light. He rolled over onto his stomach and started crawling into a small space between two rocks.

Suddenly, the ground shook. Rocks splintered and a gust of wind whooshed by. Looking back, Felix saw the passage collapse behind him. He crawled faster and faster, worming his way deeper into the field of boulders. The path went down, made a sudden turn, and then went down again. It grew black like a tunnel and then suddenly there was nothing above him but gray sky. He had come out in the open.

The monster was only a dozen yards up the path. Seeing Felix, it turned to face him, its hooves churning the gravel.

Felix wanted very, very badly to wake up. Unfortunately, he had no idea how to do that. He turned to run, knowing that the monster could run faster.

Then he heard a sound that was not made by a monster.

"Hey! Get out of here!"

It sounded like a boy.

Listening, the monster turned sideways. The voice was coming from the path above it. With the monster between them, Felix couldn't see the boy.

"Go on, get!" shouted the voice. The voice sounded strangely familiar.

The monster looked up the path. Then it looked down the path, at Felix. It hesitated.

"I said *get!*" came a shout, louder than before, echoing off the towering cliff above them.

Suddenly, the monster bolted like a sheep chased by a dog. It ran straight at Felix. With no time to move out of the way, Felix crouched down and covered his head, waiting to be squished into jelly.

But at the last second, the monster veered off the path. Rocks skidded and broke. Trees cracked and fell. The monster's roars were replaced by squeals of fear. Felix watched as it pinballed through the boulder field and into the forest. He listened as the sounds of its flight echoed away into silence.

Then Felix turned around.

"Hello?" he called.

A whistled tune answered. Felix knew the song: it was called "Over the Rainbow."

And then a boy walked out from behind a rock. He came down the path and stopped in front of Felix.

Felix looked at the boy, flabbergasted. The boy had orange hair and fair skin, just like Felix. The boy was the same size as Felix, too. In fact, from the tuft of hair sticking up on the back of his head to the small white scar on his lip, the boy looked in every way just like Felix. If the other boy had been wearing pajamas and a bathrobe, not jeans and a flannel shirt, Felix would have felt as though he were staring into a mirror.

The boy was looking at Felix curiously, too.

"Did you really chase that monster away?" asked Felix.

"It wasn't a very big monster," said the boy.

"It's the biggest monster I've ever seen," said Felix. "How did you do it?"

The boy shook his head. "It's my turn to ask you a question. Where did you come from?"

"From my bedroom," said Felix. "I'm dreaming this."

The other boy laughed. "That's funny."

A faraway roar rolled up the mountain and the boy looked down the trail.

"We'd better go," he said. "We don't want to be here when he comes back with his friends."

"Friends?" said Felix. "He has friends?"

"Well, I've never seen them playing together. But there are a bunch more monsters and sometimes they all show up in the same place."

The other orange-haired boy turned and started climbing up the trail.

"What's your name?" asked Felix.

"Felix," said the boy. "Come on, let's go."

SIX

They made their way back up to the ridge and then climbed down into the valley. The woods again grew thick and dark and the trees rose high overhead. Thickets of thornbushes pressed in close and spiny branches stretched across the path.

Felix was watching the rising and falling sneakers of the Other Felix on the trail when, suddenly, he felt a sting and cried out. He stopped. A sharp black thorn tugged at his sleeve. Gently unsnagging himself, he rolled back his sleeve and looked. Dark red blood oozed from a deep puncture. Felix blinked back tears.

The Other Felix was beside him, looking. "Press

your thumb against it, hard," he said. "We have to keep going."

Felix pressed the thumb of his left hand against the wound and stumbled forward. It was hard to keep his balance on the sloping path without moving his arms.

Ahead of him, the Other Felix was looking left and right as he walked. Every now and then he would turn and walk a few steps backward, looking down the trail behind them.

"They eat kids, you know," said the Other Felix.

Felix shuddered. "Have they eaten anyone you know?"

"I'm the only kid here. But I've seen bones of kids. So they must have eaten some other kids, a long time ago. And they're always hungry."

"The monster I saw was scared of you," said Felix.

"Well, I surprised him. I'm pretty good at fighting them, but sometimes, when they calm down, they remember that they're nine-hundred-pound monsters and I'm only a nine-year-old boy."

"How many monsters are there?"

"A lot. Sometimes I see new ones, too."

"Where are we going?"

"To the tower. I live there."

"Is it safe?"

34

"Pretty safe."

The Other Felix turned back up the trail and quickened his pace. Felix followed, breathing hard. They walked and walked, going down and down. After what seemed like hours, they reached the valley floor. There were fewer thornbushes, and the trees were shaggy with moss. Sometimes the moss was dark green and as long as a horse's tail, and sometimes it was bright green and thin as paper.

There were clearings in the trees, some of them floored with packed, bare earth, and some of them filled with black, brackish water. Mushrooms grew on the ground and on the sides of trees, some of them nearly a foot across. Once in a while Felix heard the clicking of a bug or the lonely chirp of a bird.

Then he heard rushing water. It was faint at first, but as they walked, the sound grew louder and louder. Soon he had to raise his voice to speak.

"Is that a river? I've never seen a real river—one that didn't have concrete sides, I mean."

The Other Felix laughed and shook his head. "You'll see."

In a few minutes the trees fell away on the left and right and a river rushed past, as wide as three city streets, brown and foaming. Striking hidden rocks, it leaped into the air, or whirled around, or saddled and bucked up again.

A wooden raft bobbed in the water. It was tethered to a thick wire that ran from the near shore to the far shore. Felix had seen something like it in one of Mrs. Nowak's books. The wire was supposed to guide the raft across the river and keep it from getting washed downstream. But the water was so rough that Felix felt sure the wire would break.

The Other Felix climbed onto the raft. He balanced himself against its rocking motion and lifted a slack rope out of the water.

"Come on," he said.

Felix looked at the raft, worried. It was made of logs hammered together with big iron nails. The logs were wet and slimy, and the nails were red with rust.

Behind them, in the woods, there was a roar.

Felix climbed onto the raft. He couldn't keep his balance standing up, so he knelt down on the logs. His pants got wet, and his knees got knocked, but he didn't think he would fall into the water.

The Other Felix pulled on the rope and the raft slipped out into the current. Felix could feel the river pushing them as if it wanted to throw them downstream. But the Other Felix kept pulling and, steadily, the raft moved across the river.

A few minutes later, they climbed onto the

opposite bank. The Other Felix wound a rope around a tree trunk, tying the raft tight.

"Can the monsters get over the river?" asked Felix.

"Monsters can go anywhere," said the Other Felix.

Felix gulped. His stomach felt cold and hollow. He followed the Other Felix into the woods.

In a little while they arrived at the biggest clearing yet, the size of a soccer field. In the middle of the clearing, a tower built from rough wooden logs rose three stories high. Its nail-studded door was shut and the windows on the first floor were tightly shuttered. The windows on the second floor were tall, narrow slits. On the third floor there were normal-sized windows, though they didn't have glass in them.

The Other Felix led Felix to the tower door. A strip of leather was threaded through a small hole near the top of the door. The Other Felix tugged the strip. There was a groan of rubbing wood and the Other Felix pushed the door open. Felix followed him inside.

The leather strip was attached to a hinged plank on the back of the door. The Other Felix closed the door and lowered the plank into a bracket, barring the door again. Then he pulled the leather strip out of the hole, locking the door from the inside. Except for the thin lines of light stealing around the shuttered windows, the room was dark.

"How did you find this place?" asked Felix.

"It's always been here," said the Other Felix.

"But how long have you been here?"

"I've always been here, too. How many more questions are you going to ask?"

"A lot," said Felix. "If the monsters can go anywhere, then they can come here, too. Can they even come inside?"

"No, not inside."

"Why not?"

"The door's too small. They won't fit. Well, most of them won't."

"But they might wait outside, right? What happens when we need to go outside?"

"I'm tired of answering questions," said the Other Felix.

The Other Felix struck a match. It flared and seemed to go out. Then, slowly, the flame grew. In the darkness, Felix could see crumpled balls of paper catching fire. The flames grew brighter and he could see them lighting the belly of an old iron stove. Twigs crackled and soon fire filled the stove's belly. The Other Felix fed in some bigger sticks and a short log and then closed the door. He used a glowing twig to light a lantern with a glass chimney. The room took on an amber glow. The corners were dark, but Felix could see a table with two chairs, a toy chest, a bookcase filled with books, a bow and some arrows, and an ax.

"How did you learn to light a fire?" asked Felix, curious. "My mom and dad would never let me light a fire."

The Other Felix shrugged. "I learned it from a book." He took a paper bag down from a shelf near the stove. He offered the bag to Felix. In the bag were two sandwiches, two apples, and two cookies. Felix took one of each. He gave the bag back.

The Other Felix dragged two beanbag chairs out of a dark corner and put them in front of the stove. The boys sat down and started eating. The sandwich was peanut butter and jelly on soft brown bread with potato chips smooshed into it. It was delicious. Felix ate it hungrily. Then he ate the apple, all of it except the stem and the seeds and the little fuzzy thing on the bottom. Then he ate the cookie. It had oatmeal and peanut butter and chocolate chips and was the best thing of all.

The Other Felix took a steel canteen off a peg on the wall and gave it to Felix. The water inside was cold and had a clean, rocky taste, as though it had been running through a cave underground. He drank thirstily, then lay back before the fire. Watching the flames dance in the grate, he realized that he was getting sleepy. He yawned.

"Is your name really Felix?" asked Felix.

"Yes," said the Other Felix.

"That's my name, too."

"It is?"

"Yes. So it feels funny to call you Felix," said Felix.

"Well," said the Other Felix, "how do you think I feel?"

"That's a good point," said Felix. "Nice to meet you, Felix."

"Nice to meet you, too, Felix," said the Other Felix.

They both laughed. And then, warm and tired, Felix fell asleep.

SEVEN

Felix woke to the clattering sound of his window
shade going up. His mother was already dressed
for work. She sipped coffee as she stepped carefully
over the toys on the floor of his room.

"Wake up, lazybones," she said. "Time to go to
school."

Felix blinked in the sunlight. With each blink,
his mother was farther across the room. He blinked
once more and she was gone. He yawned and
stretched himself into a more comfortable position.
He took a deep breath and let it out slowly. He
wasn't tired. His heart wasn't racing. He had slept
through the night, even though he had dreamed.

He smiled.

Then he sat up and slid out of bed.

When he got to school he stopped smiling. Chase, big as a mountain, was already sitting at the desk by the window. Chase stared at Felix with hard, flinty eyes. Felix looked down. He watched his shoes crossing the pebbly brown linoleum tiles. He sat down in his chair and turned to face the front of the room. He didn't look over at Chase all day.

After recess, Miss Olu asked the kids to open their workbooks for math. While they were doing this, she went to the materials cabinet and took out the bin of calculators. She walked from desk to desk, giving one calculator to each student.

When she got to Felix and Chase, she frowned. There was only one calculator left.

"What's wrong?" asked Felix, even though he knew.

"We are missing one calculator," said Miss Olu.

"That's weird," said Chase.

Felix finally looked at Chase. Chase was wearing a puzzled expression on his face. He looked very honest.

"We are missing one *particular* calculator," said Miss Olu. "The one that belongs to desk number twenty-nine."

"How do you know?" asked Felix.

"Before I handed out the calculators for the first time, I put a number on the back of each one."

Felix hadn't noticed the numbers. He had assumed that Chase had stolen his own calculator. But desk number twenty-nine was Felix's desk, and the missing calculator was his.

Miss Olu gave the last calculator to Chase. Chase said thank you, which was new. He looked at Felix, his eyebrows raised.

"Do you know what happened to your calculator?" Miss Olu asked Felix.

Felix thought for a moment. Though he didn't want to be a tattletale, he didn't want Miss Olu to think he would steal, either. But before he could say anything, Chase answered for him.

"Felix took it," said Chase. "I didn't want to say anything, but he did. I saw him take it after school."

"Felix, is this true?" asked Miss Olu.

"No!" said Felix. "No, it's not!"

Miss Olu frowned at both of them. "We will get to the bottom of this," she said. "Right now you will have to share."

Felix wanted to get as far away from Chase as he could, and now they had to scoot their desks together. With the calculator resting half on Chase's desk, half on Felix's, Felix could feel Chase's hot breath on his arm. He rubbed it, but it wasn't like he could rub off breathing.

He thought about hitting Chase, but Chase was so much bigger than him. Besides, Felix had never hit anybody.

Chase made a big deal about pushing the buttons for the first problem, but after that he lost interest. He had stolen Felix's calculator and made Miss Olu think that Felix was the thief, but he didn't really seem to care about calculators at all. Felix did the second problem, and the third one, too. Before long, the calculator was all the way on Felix's desk, and Chase was drawing pictures in his workbook.

When Felix walked outside after school, he was surprised to see his mother coming toward him. She was talking on the phone and watching her feet on the uneven paving stones.

She almost ran over him. Raising an eyebrow, she stopped, said good-bye, and folded her phone shut.

"I didn't see you, Felix," she said. "Why didn't you say anything?"

"I was standing right in front of you," said Felix.

"Anyway, I just called Mrs. Nowak and told her you weren't coming. It was slow at work, so they let me off early. I thought we could all go out to dinner."

"Dad, too?" asked Felix.

"Dad, too," said his mother.

Felix smiled. They didn't eat dinner in restaurants very often.

"But he won't be able to meet us for a while," said his mother. "Do you want to go to the park?"

Felix did. They started walking, squinting into the falling sun. A breeze stirred the dry leaves in the gutters, some of them brown or yellow or orange, some of them green.

At the park, there were only little kids, no one Felix's age. Felix's mother sat down on a bench and took out her phone again. Felix walked slowly over to the swings. He swung for a while, pumping his legs and leaning back, feeling the pleasant drop in his stomach as he fell back toward the ground. The swings were not very tall, and it was easy for him to swing so high that the chain went slack at the top.

After a while he got tired of swinging and stopped pumping his legs. He went back and forth, each swing a little shorter. He looked at his mother. She was still talking on the phone. She didn't see him looking.

He let go of the chains and jumped out of the swing. He looked at his mother again and then walked farther into the park.

It was a small park, nestled between two apartment buildings. In addition to the swings and a jungle gym, there was a large circle where, in summer, concrete turtles sprayed water for kids to splash in. There were sidewalks and short walls and little hills in the corners. There were almost enough bushes and trees to pretend it was a forest.

Felix circled the park, climbing up and down the hills. He found a broken bottle under a bush, its jagged glass shimmering like green jewels. Being very careful not to touch the sharp parts, he picked up the bottle by its neck. The neck was sticky. There was a paper label attached to it, and stuck to the paper label were different-sized triangles of glass.

"Better be careful!"

Startled, Felix dropped the bottle. It hit a rock and broke into smaller pieces.

There was a man in the bush, lying in a sleeping bag on a big piece of cardboard. The man's hair was dark and tangled, and one eye was milky white.

"That's glass, kid," said the man.

"I know," said Felix.

"I know 'cause I put it there."

Felix thought he should probably run. But the man, propped up on one elbow, didn't move. So Felix didn't move, either.

"You shouldn't litter," said Felix.

"Accident," said the man. "I dropped it. You got a mom?"

Felix nodded his head up and down.

"Where is she? Why isn't she watching you?"

"She is. She's over there," said Felix, pointing.

The man squinted with his one good eye. He saw Felix's mother. He nodded.

"That's good," said the man. "Sometimes it's not safe in the park."

"Are you afraid, sleeping out here?" asked Felix.

Now the man nodded his head. "Sometimes. Yeah, you guessed it. Sometimes I am."

"Well, what do you do when you're afraid?"

"I just deal with it. There's no magic to make it go away. But then, after a while, sometimes I forget I'm afraid."

"I have to go," Felix told the man.

"See you later, kid," said the man.

Felix walked back to his mother. She was still talking on the phone.

"When are we going to have dinner?" he asked, interrupting.

"In a little while. Keep playing."

Even the little kids had left the park. Felix and his mother and the strange man were the only ones left. Felix went to a nearby triangle of trees and,

after looking carefully for broken glass, sat down in the grass. He sat there until the streetlights came on.

Finally, he was too cold to sit any longer. His ears were sore and his nose was dripping. He zipped his jacket up to the top and went over to his mother. She had folded her phone closed. She was frowning.

"I'm hungry," said Felix.

"Me, too," said his mother. "But your dad keeps getting held up."

"I'm cold, too," said Felix. "I'm even colder than I am hungry. I want to go to the restaurant."

His mother looked around them at the empty park. The shadows of branches were like long, stiff fingers.

"You're right," she said. "We can't wait all night. Let's go."

"All right!" said Felix.

"Don't forget your backpack."

Felix looked. He had left his backpack in the triangle of trees. Even though the trees weren't too close to the strange man, he ran all the way there and all the way back.

They walked to a Mexican restaurant where they were the only customers. Felix's mother ordered a big green drink with salt clumped around the rim of the glass. Felix wasn't allowed to drink soda, and

the restaurant didn't have milk or apple juice, so he just drank water. Together they ate a big basket of salted chips. Felix's mother dipped them in the salsa. The salsa was too hot for Felix, so he ate the chips dry, wishing the restaurant had some that wasn't so spicy.

"So, how was school?" asked Felix's mother.

Felix chewed carefully, pretending that his mouth was too full to talk. He was trying to decide whether to tell her about Chase and the calculator. But what if she didn't believe him, either?

"School was fine," he said.

"Fine, huh? Was it very fine or only sort of fine? Were some parts more fine than others?"

"It was all kind of medium fine. So, how was work?"

Felix's mother laughed. She took a sip of her big green drink. She shook her head. "Work was fine."

"Do you like working with kids?"

"Of course I do."

"Even sick kids?"

"Most of the kids I see are sick."

"And some of them die," said Felix.

Felix's mother sipped her big green drink again. "Yes, some of them die."

"Have you ever seen a dead kid?" he asked.

"Yes. It was the saddest thing I ever saw."

"What happens to kids who die?"

His mother hesitated. "Well, their bodies—"

"I don't mean that," interrupted Felix. "I know their bodies go to the graveyard. But what happens to . . . *them?*"

"Nobody knows exactly what happens to people after they die," said his mother. "But they live on in our thoughts. And in our dreams."

Felix wondered if the Other Felix was a dead kid who had come to live in his dreams. Maybe lots of kids had dreamland friends, too. But that didn't seem right. If the Other Felix was dead, why did he look exactly like Felix and have the same name?

After they had eaten all the chips, Felix's mother sighed and looked at her watch. She waved the waiter over and asked to order. The food came quickly: a whole piece of fish, with the head still on it, for Felix's mother, and bean-and-cheese quesa-dillas for Felix. They were just about done eating when the door opened and Felix's father walked in.

"Sorry I'm late," he said, picking up a menu.

"How was work?" asked Felix.

Felix's father looked at him. Then he looked at Felix's mother. Then he looked at the big green drink in front of her.

"I'll have one of those," he said.

• • •

Felix wandered around the empty restaurant while his parents talked and ate. It looked as though there had been a party years ago that had never been cleaned up. Faded red-white-and-green flags hung from strings crisscrossing the ceiling. Dusty piñatas decorated the walls. Shrunken balloons, their helium long since leaked out, dangled from strings.

It felt like the middle of the night. Felix was bored and wanted to go home. He sat down at an empty table near his parents and put his head down on his arms.

". . . and meanwhile, we're left twisting in the wind," said Felix's father. "After all this work, we're going to meet our deadline, but now I'm worried that New York is going to ask for a completely new set of deliverables. New York and L.A. won't talk to each other, but they'll talk to us, and they're both telling us completely different things. At the end of the month, we'll lose our funding unless Capstan recommits—and, frankly, I'm not sure they should. But if they don't, we're dead in the water."

Felix lifted his head off the table. "What's a 'deliverable'?" he asked.

His parents stopped talking and looked at him.

"It's . . . something you're supposed to deliver," said Felix's father. He smiled, but his smile seemed tired.

"But what, exactly?" asked Felix. "What deliverables are you supposed to deliver?"

"Design documents. Grown-up stuff."

"Does this mean the Project is in trouble?" asked Felix.

Felix's parents looked at each other.

"Well, it's not going great," said his father.

"It's going to be just fine," said his mother.

"What happens if we're dead in the water?" asked Felix.

"It's going to be just fine," repeated his mother.

Felix was tired when they finally got home. He dropped his backpack on the floor and lay down on the bed wearing his clothes. His mother told him to put on his pajamas. When he didn't move, she pulled off his shirt, grunting and groaning and making a joke out of it. Suddenly, she stopped.

"That cut on your arm," she said, "did you get it on the playground?"

Felix looked down at the place where he'd been pricked by a thorn.

"No," he said.

His mother didn't believe him. Even though it was already scabbed over, she told him it might get infected. She got cotton balls and rubbing alcohol and scrubbed it until it hurt all over again. Then she put a Band-Aid on it. Felix, still sleepy, just lay there, wincing.

When she was done doctoring him, his mother told him again to put on his pajamas. When he didn't move, she shook her head and stood up.

"Fine, but you'll be cold if you don't put them on."

After she left, he did get cold. Yawning, he sat up and pulled the pajama top over his head. Then he dangled his feet over the edge of the bed and pulled on the pants.

Felix's father came to the door. "Want a story tonight, Felix?"

"No," said Felix.

"Good night, then," said his father, clicking off the light.

Felix lay down and pulled up the covers. He was so tired that he forgot to be afraid of monsters.

EIGHT

Felix woke up in the beanbag chair. He was shivering. The belly of the stove was cold and empty. Morning light peeped in around the edges of the shutters and through the cracks between the logs of the tower's walls. The Other Felix was gone.

In one corner of the room, a ladder led to a square cut into the ceiling. Felix climbed up the ladder to the second floor. The room above had four narrow windows, two beds, a clothes dresser, and a bookshelf full of old-looking books. Felix read the spines on several of the books. One was called *How to Hunt* and another was called *How to Sleep*. In the opposite corner, another ladder led up to another trapdoor in the ceiling.

He climbed the ladder to the third floor. It was completely empty. He looked out the windows. He saw stumps and rocks and puddles. He saw a green wall of trees at the edge of the clearing. And yet another ladder led up to a closed trapdoor. Felix climbed to the top of the ladder and pushed on the trapdoor. It didn't move.

Steadying himself, he pushed again. The heavy wooden trapdoor only moved a little bit. He pushed harder and it began to rise. It went straight up and over and slammed down on the roof.

Felix poked his head through the opening. Wind ruffled his hair. Very slowly, very carefully, he climbed out onto the flat tower roof. He crawled to the center and sat down. In his waking life, Felix lived at a much greater height than this—but the windows of his family's apartment were sealed shut.

He was above the trees. The sky was clear and gray-blue. It looked as if the sun was about to come up. His breath made little clouds in the air.

"Felix!" he called. His voice died over the tree-tops without even an echo.

He shouted louder. "Felix! Felix, where are you?"

A bug buzzed in his ear, but the Other Felix didn't answer.

Felix climbed down the ladder to the second

floor. He opened the dresser drawers. They were filled with neatly folded clothes. He pulled a pair of corduroy pants over his pajama pants and buttoned a flannel shirt over his pajama shirt. He put on a pair of scratchy wool socks and then put his feet back in his slippers. He went downstairs again.

The light coming through the cracks in the walls was growing brighter and warmer. He wasn't shivering anymore. But now he was hungry. He looked around the first-floor room. He found crumbs and dirty dishes but no food. His stomach growled like a little monster.

He went over to the front door. It was securely bolted, and the leather string was threaded through the hole to the outside so the Other Felix could get back in. Carefully, Felix lifted the bolt. He cracked the door and peered out.

Outside, it was sunny and warm. Green leaves steamed in the sun. Birds chirped. Insects buzzed and clicked. No monsters roared.

Felix opened the door and went outside. Shading his eyes against the bright morning sun, he could see that there were other paths leading into the woods. He went across the clearing, chose a path at random, and started walking along it. In the shade, it grew suddenly cooler. The path twisted and turned, and Felix couldn't see ahead or behind. The earth was wet and his slippers filled with mud.

Suddenly, the birds stopped singing. The air was quiet.

Something was coming, crashing through the brush, coming down the trail toward him. Felix tried to remember what the Other Felix had done to make the monster run away.

The crashing sounds grew louder and came toward him faster. Terrified, Felix turned to run.

Then the noise stopped. Wincing, Felix turned back around.

The Other Felix stood on the trail in front of him, grinning. Over one shoulder he carried a fishing pole. Over the other shoulder he carried a string of fish filets. In his shirt pocket was a greasy bag of french fries. Poking out of a fishing creel were two bottles of soda. Felix wondered where the Other Felix had caught and cooked the fish. They were breaded and crispy, just the way he liked.

"Are you hungry?" asked the Other Felix, cheerfully.

Felix nodded his head up and down.

"Then let's have a picnic."

They walked back to the clearing and sat down in the shade of a tree. The Other Felix took a handkerchief out of his creel and spread it on the ground for a tablecloth. Felix ate with gusto, getting grease and salt all over his face and fingers.

"Where did you go this morning?" asked Felix with his mouth full.

"Looking for food, like I always do," said the Other Felix. "Where did you go last night?"

"What do you mean?"

"One minute, we were eating sandwiches, and the next minute, you were gone."

"I guess I went home," said Felix.

"What's your home like?" asked the Other Felix.

It took a long time for Felix to explain what his home was like. The Other Felix had never seen a city, a high-rise, or even a car. The Other Felix didn't have a family. And he definitely didn't go to school.

Amazed at the fantastic things he was hearing, the Other Felix had stopped eating. "So how many people live in the city?" he asked.

Felix licked his fingers. He thought about asking for the Other Felix's french fries but decided that would be bad manners.

"Three million, I think. But way more than that if you count the suburbs."

"That's a lot. You're the first person I've ever seen."

"But if I'm the first person you've ever seen," said Felix, "how do you know how to speak English?"

"Maybe I learned it from a book," said the Other Felix. "I have a lot of books and they tell me how to do all sorts of things."

"But how would you read about learning to read if you didn't know how to read?"

"I don't know."

"Do you remember when you didn't know how to read, when you were little?"

"No. I don't remember being little."

"Aren't you lonely, living here?" asked Felix.

"Well, if I was, I didn't know it, because I never had a friend before."

"Does that mean we're friends?"

"I don't know. Do you?"

"Yes," said Felix. "I think we're friends."

NINE

In the morning, Felix's mother looked at his muddy slippers and just shook her head.

"I won't even ask," she said.

Felix wanted her to ask, even though he knew she would never believe what he told her. But since she didn't, he put the muddy slippers on the floor next to his dirty clothes hamper. Then he got dressed for school.

At school, Felix took off his coat and his backpack and hung them on their pegs at the back of the room. Chase came through the door and Felix hurried to his desk. He wondered when Miss Olu would find out that Chase had lied about taking the calculator. He decided to ignore Chase until she did.

Luckily, Chase ignored him, too.

The morning went fine. Felix was pretty good at spelling, so he liked that. He was pretty good at language arts, so he liked that, too. But he didn't like it when Miss Olu asked him to read aloud. When he read aloud, he didn't sound like the good reader he knew he really was. He made mistakes. He read too fast. The characters, who sounded so real in his head, all sounded like a kid named Felix.

Fortunately, today Miss Olu asked Chase to read. Chase was definitely not a good reader. He made a lot of mistakes. He said "excape" instead of "escape." He lost his place on the page. Miss Olu was patient but Chase was embarrassed. When she finally said he could stop, he closed his book and stared at the top of his desk. His face was bright, angry red.

Good, thought Felix.

Science was not so great. Miss Olu cut open a big worm and pinned it to a board.

"Big deal," said Chase. "I did that at my old school."

Then Miss Olu made the students come look at it.

"These are the earthworm's hearts, and this is its intestine," said Miss Olu.

"Yum!" said Chase.

Some of the kids laughed.

Felix could barely bring himself to look. The worm smelled funny. When he finally did look, he couldn't believe how much stuff there was inside a worm. He thought that it would look like, well, more worm. But there were lots of specific parts.

Suddenly, he felt dizzy and wondered if he was going to throw up. He went back to his seat and put his head down on his desk.

Then, at lunch, the lunch lady served spaghetti and meatballs. Chase ate with his fingers, dangling the noodles out of his mouth.

"Worms!" He picked up a meatball. "And worm poop!"

The kids at Chase's table thought he was very funny. Some of them imitated him, trying to get him to laugh.

Sitting alone, Felix ate his carrots and his buttered bread and his pears. Every time he looked at the noodles and the meatballs he was reminded of worms and his stomach felt funny. He wondered if there were any parts inside a spaghetti noodle.

At recess, Felix was sitting on the teeter-totter

when a kid named Archie climbed on the other end. They made a game of pushing off as hard as they could and bouncing out of their seats. Archie was better at it. Felix had to hold on tight to the handle to keep from flying off completely.

The other kids were playing chase with Chase. They ran in a screaming pack, under and around the jungle gym, until a girl named Soledad hit her head on the bottom of the slide and started crying. The recess teacher rushed over and all the kids crowded around. When the teacher helped Soledad up, everyone could see that her head was bleeding.

Archie caught his breath as he fell back into his seat.

"I don't want to play with Chase," he said.

"Me neither," said Felix.

Felix pushed with his legs and waited for the bump.

Before math class, Miss Olu told Chase and Felix to step out into the hall. She closed the door behind them. The hall was darker than the classroom because there were no windows. It felt strange to be in the hall without a hundred noisy kids being there, too. At the end of the hall, Mr. Lee, the custodian, plunked a mop into a mop bucket and then wrung it out.

"I need to know the truth about what happened to the calculator," said Miss Olu.

"It was Felix," said Chase. "I already told you that."

"But he denied it," said Miss Olu. "Felix, is this true?"

As Miss Olu's eyes turned to him, Felix decided that he would tell her, after all. She didn't seem to believe Chase, and she would probably find out the truth on her own. So there was nothing wrong with telling her what she practically almost already knew.

"No," he said.

"I saw him," insisted Chase. "Look in his backpack."

"Chase, please be quiet. I am talking to Felix," said Miss Olu. "Felix, do you have something to tell me?"

Felix cleared his throat to speak again. But Chase, standing just behind Miss Olu, scowled and made a fist. Felix suddenly wondered whether it would be worse to be punished by Miss Olu or to be punched by Chase. Looking into Miss Olu's kind eyes, he decided that her punishment would be easier. He shook his head.

"I suppose I will have to see for myself," said Miss Olu.

Miss Olu made them sit on benches on opposite sides of the hall. Then she went into the room. When she opened the door they could hear the kids talking. Miss Olu shushed them and closed the door behind her. Chase made a fist again and slapped it into the palm of his other hand. The sound echoed down the hallway. Felix looked away, holding on to the bench so his hands wouldn't shake. Still, even if he didn't say anything, in a moment Miss Olu would know that Chase had told a terrible lie.

The door opened again and Miss Olu came out, holding Felix's backpack. She unzipped it and looked inside. Then she reached in and pulled out the calculator.

TEN

Felix wasn't afraid of going to sleep anymore. At night, he put on his pajamas and brushed his teeth without waiting for his mother to remind him. He read a chapter from his book and then allowed his parents to read him one. Then he yawned and asked them to turn out the light. He told them that he was feeling sleepy, or that he had had a full day. His parents looked at him, or each other, with raised eyebrows. He used to ask them to read another chapter, and then another. But now they said good night, and soon he was lying quietly in the dark.

Then he smiled and closed his eyes.

When he woke up in the wooden tower, he would quickly change into some of the Other

Felix's clothes. Then he would climb down the ladder and go looking for the Other Felix. Sometimes he found him right away. Other times he had to look for a while. But the Other Felix always turned up eventually. Felix was getting less and less afraid of the forest. Sometimes he heard monsters roaring in the distance but so far the monsters had stayed out of sight.

The Other Felix knew everything that Felix did not. He knew how to find food and how to cook it. He knew how to knot a rope, how to start a fire, and how to climb a tree. He knew how to swim. Felix thought that the Other Felix would grow tired of teaching him, but every night, which was a whole day in the dreamland, Felix learned something new.

He learned how to hunt. The Other Felix showed him how to set snares for birds and squirrels, and how to stun a rabbit with a stone. He taught him how to look for animals and how to wait, silent and unmoving, until the animals forgot that the boys were different from the rocks and trees of the forest.

Felix was happy to eat the birds, squirrels, and rabbits once the Other Felix had cooked them. But he still wasn't ready to do the messy, bloody work himself. Watching the Other Felix pluck feathers from a scrawny bird, he lost his appetite.

"That's disgusting," said Felix.

"You ate some last night," said the Other Felix.

"But that was food. This is just a dead bird."

"Food is almost always something before it's food."

"When my mom buys chicken, it's wrapped in plastic. And it's clean."

"Really? Well, I bet someone had to clean it and cut it and wrap it."

Felix thought about that. The Other Felix was right. But Felix still didn't want to be the one to do the dirty work.

"What if I wasn't here?" asked the Other Felix. "Would you just go hungry?"

"I'd look for peanut-butter-and-jelly sandwiches," said Felix.

"I find those sometimes," said the Other Felix. "But I don't know who makes them."

When they weren't hunting, they played. They played tag and hide-and-seek. They ran races and played catch. They played marbles. And when the sun went down, they told each other scary stories. The Other Felix's stories were so scary that Felix was afraid of falling asleep, in case he had a nightmare. But he was already asleep, already dreaming. When he fell asleep in the dreamland, he woke up in his own bed. He always took care to change out of the Other Felix's clothes before falling asleep—if he woke up in someone else's clothes, it would have been difficult to explain to his mother.

One day, Felix found the Other Felix carrying a bow. A half-dozen arrows were sticking out of a quiver slung over his shoulder.

"Where did you get the bow?" asked Felix.

"I made it," said the Other Felix.

"Will you show me how?"

"It takes a while."

"I've got plenty of time," said Felix.

It took a week. The Other Felix showed him how to find the right kind of tree, how to select the right branch, and how to cut it off with a jagged-toothed saw. After peeling the bark from the branch and rubbing the wood smooth, they set off on an overgrown path. They walked and walked for so long that Felix was afraid they would see monsters.

Indeed, the Other Felix put his finger to his lips, and they walked along in silence, listening. The trees thinned and the path climbed around rocks. Then, suddenly, a thin curtain of mist drifted toward them. As they walked forward, the mist grew thicker until it was almost a fog. It swirled slowly in the breeze. Then it cleared, and Felix saw dark pools of water cupped in rocky crags at the bottom of a cliff. The pools steamed.

69

"There are usually monsters here," whispered the Other Felix. "But we need the hot water."

It was a dismal place. Beside the nearest pool, the ground had been trampled flat. Damp, woolly hanks of fur lay matted on the ground and snagged on thorny branches. Felix dipped his fingers in the water. The water was as hot as a bath. The Other Felix was taking off his clothes.

"Might as well get clean while we're here," he said.

The Other Felix put his feet into the water and gradually lowered himself in. He brought the bow stick in, too, and held it underwater.

"We have to get it good and soaking," said the Other Felix. "It might take a while."

Felix watched the trees, afraid the monsters would appear. But after a while, the water was too tempting. Felix took off his clothes. At first, he sat on the cool rocks with his feet in the hot water. Then he slid in all the way to his neck. Under his feet, the rocks were slick and slimy. The hot water made him sweat. It felt good.

The two of them crouched in the water, watching the forest and listening.

"Are there monsters where you come from?" asked the Other Felix.

"Not really," said Felix. "There are wild

animals, and there are bad people, but they're different from monsters."

"And there are lots of kids?"

"Millions of them. Billions even."

"It sounds wonderful."

"It's okay," said Felix. "But I like it here better."

The Other Felix looked surprised. "Really?"

Felix nodded his head. "Really."

"Will you stay here?"

"I don't think I can. I don't know how."

"But you'll always come back, right?"

"I hope so."

"I hope so, too."

After a while, the Other Felix said that the bow had soaked long enough. They climbed out, their skin pink and wrinkled, and pulled their dry clothes onto their wet bodies. Then they made their way back down the trail, feeling safer with every step.

Now the wood was soft enough to bend. Back at the tower, the Other Felix showed Felix how to find the curve of the stick and how to shape it into a bow with a knife. It was slow work. Night after night Felix carved the bow, sometimes stopping to sharpen the knife on a whetstone, until the thick middle part made a handle that felt good to hold and the two ends were thinner and more easily bent.

Then the Other Felix showed him how to make

arrows. They searched the forest floor for long, straight sticks. When they had found several, they peeled off the bark and whittled them until they were the same width all the way along. The Other Felix straightened them over a fire.

Then, carefully, they cut three long slits at one end of each shaft. They cut feathers in half, lengthwise, and slid them into the slits. Unraveling thread from their own clothes, they used the thread to tie the feathers into the shafts.

"The feathers on the arrow are called fletchings," said the Other Felix.

Felix thought it was a funny word, but he liked knowing it.

Finally, they carved sharp points on the ends of the arrows and hardened them in the fire. Now Felix had his own bow and his own arrows. But something was missing.

"What do I use for a bowstring?" he asked the Other Felix.

The Other Felix reached in his pocket. Smiling, he took out something skinny and tangled and brown.

"I already made you one," he said. "I used old shoelaces."

Felix bent the bow and the Other Felix fitted the string over the ends. When he was done, Felix let go and the bow, instead of springing back to its original shape, stayed bent, with the shoelace bow-string pulled taut.

"Now you need to learn how to shoot it," said the Other Felix.

They stuffed an old red-checked shirt full of dry grass and tied it to a tree at the edge of the clearing. Standing with their backs to the tree, they counted off thirty steps. They turned around. The Other Felix went first, pulling an arrow from his quiver and fit-ting it to his bow, then pulling the string back to his ear. He closed one eye, aimed, and let go.

The bow went *thwip!* and the arrow darted through the air and stuck into the shirt.

Felix went next. With his right hand, he fitted the nock of an arrow into the string and rested the shaft against the thumb of his left hand. He pulled the string back. It was harder than it looked, and by the time the bow was bent, his arms were trem-bling. He pointed the arrow's tip at the stuffed shirt and let go of the bowstring. The feathers scraped his hand as they went past. The arrow sailed to one side, hit a rock on the ground, skipped up in the air—and floated lazily to the ground.

Felix dropped the bow and put his thumb in his mouth. It felt like he had a rug burn.

The Other Felix laughed. "Well, at least you didn't shoot yourself in the foot," he said.

Felix looked at the Other Felix's arrow sticking out of the shirt. He thought that it would be a long time before he would be able to hunt for dinner—or fight off a monster.

"You'll get better if you practice," said the Other Felix. "Bows aren't any good against monsters anyway."

It was almost as if the Other Felix could read his thoughts.

ELEVEN

A week had gone by since Miss Olu had found the calculator in his backpack, but Felix felt as though he was still being punished. After scolding him and telling him how disappointed she was in him, she had made him sit on a bench in the hall for the whole math class. Even though she hadn't told the other kids why, they all knew the reason. And so, instead of that being the end of his punishment, it was only the beginning.

The next day, when Jory Clements was showing his new trading cards to kids on the playground, he let all the kids hold them except Felix. As if Felix would ever want to steal a bunch of crummy trading cards. As if he had ever wanted to steal a calculator!

At story time, Miss Olu read the first two chapters of a new book. The book was a mystery about a girl detective who had to help the grown-ups find a thief.

While she read, Chase folded lines into a piece of paper so he could tear the corner off quietly. Hiding the paper with his hand, he wrote something on it. Then he folded the paper into a tiny square, dropped it on the floor, and pushed it forward with his toe. Alex Lloyd saw it and picked it up. He unfolded the note and read it. He turned around in his chair and looked at Felix. Then he folded it up again.

Felix watched as the note made its way up and down the rows of desks until it finally reached Archie. Archie read the note and then carefully, quietly, tore it into tiny pieces.

On the playground, during recess, Felix asked Archie what the note had said.

"It said, 'The theif is Felix, pass it on,'" said Archie. "But I'm pretty sure he spelled *thief* wrong."

"Thanks for tearing it up," said Felix.

"You're welcome," said Archie.

Felix was glad that not all of the kids had seen the note. But when Casper Greenblatt asked him whether he stole because his family was poor, he realized that it didn't really matter. Now *Felix* meant *thief.*

Every time Felix saw Chase, he got a stomach-ache. And he saw Chase every day.

That night, Felix was in bed listening to his mother read when he heard the front door close. His father was home. There was a swishing sound as his father shrugged out of his windbreaker. Then the closet door rumbled open and the coat hangers jangled. His father walked into the dining room and dropped his bag on the table with a thud.

"Felix, are you even listening to the story?" asked his mother.

Felix shook his head. "When someone does something bad to you, are you allowed to do something bad to them?"

"No," said his mother. "If someone does something bad to you, you should get help, from me or your father, or from your teacher. Did something happen at school?"

Felix shook his head again. He wanted to know the answer, but he didn't want to worry his parents. They had enough worries of their own.

"But why can't you do something bad back?" he asked.

"Well, you just can't. If someone hits you and you hit them, it'll never solve anything. You'll just keep hitting each other until you're black-and-blue."

"But if someone knows you'll hit them back, won't they be afraid to hit you next time?"

Felix's mother sighed. His father came to the door.

"You want to take this one?" asked his mother.

"This one what?" asked his father.

"A moral quandary."

Felix's father smiled his lopsided smile. "Out of the frying pan, into the fire. Hello, Felix."

Felix's mother told Felix good night and gave him a kiss. She stood up and kissed his father, too. Then she went out.

Felix's father sat down on the bed.

"How was work?" asked Felix.

"I went in early, I came home late, I worked at a computer all day. For lunch I ate a microwaved burrito."

"That's not the joke," said Felix. "How was work?"

"Sorry. Another day, another IOU," said his father.

"What's an IOU?"

"That's when, instead of giving you money,

someone gives you a piece of paper that says 'I owe you' the money."

"So they still owe you a dime?" asked Felix, smiling.

"They owe me a lot of dimes," said his father. "Now tell me about your quandary."

"What's a quandary?" asked Felix.

"When you're in a quandary," said his father, "you don't know what to do."

"Have you ever had a quandary?"

"Life is a quandary. We do what we think is right, and if we're wrong, we try again."

"That's a funny word," said Felix. "How do you spell it?"

"G–O–O–D N–I–G–H–T," said his father.

Felix's father pulled the covers up and tucked Felix in snugly. Then he turned out the light.

TWELVE

When Felix woke up in his dream, the Other Felix wasn't there. He got out of bed and got dressed. Then he climbed down the ladder, took his bow and arrows off their pegs, and unbolted the door and went outside. It was a cool, cloudy day.

The red-checked shirt was still tied to the tree. Felix counted thirty steps and stopped. It looked very far away, so he took five steps closer, then five more, before he felt ready to shoot. He nocked an arrow, bent the bow, and aimed. The arrow flew straight but not far enough, sticking in the ground in front of the tree. He nocked another arrow and shot again. This one flew fast and far but went too far to the right. It glanced off a tree and sailed side-ways along the edge of the clearing.

Felix's hands stung, but he was determined not to give up. He nocked his last arrow and pulled the string to his ear. He took his time aiming at the target. He breathed in and out, then waited to draw his next breath. He was sure this arrow would hit the mark. He let go.

The arrow flashed past the shirt, missing by inches, and disappeared into the woods.

Sighing, Felix collected his first two arrows, then went into the woods to search for the third. He walked twenty steps, then thirty, his eyes on the ground. After forty steps, he stopped. He didn't think his arrow could have flown this far. But where was it? He looked from side to side, wondering if the arrow had bounced in some unlikely direction.

A branch cracked, loud as a gunshot.

Felix froze. He searched the underbrush with his eyes. The busy patterns of light and shade made him feel as though he couldn't see anything. But his skin prickled.

Then, in a thick tangle of bushes, he saw something rough and cracked like the dried bed of an ancient lake. As his eyes adjusted, he saw a dark shape, rising like a mountain, with pointed, armored plates along the ridgeline. They rose and fell gently, as if the mountain was breathing. Then he saw an eye. It was dark and shiny and low to the ground. It was looking right at him.

He heard a *whuff!* and the monster moved, turning toward him and rising up, flattening the bushes, making the trunks of the trees groan in protest. It was tall and wide. It blocked out the sun.

The monster's mouth opened. Felix saw rows and rows of broad, flat teeth and a wet purple tongue. He saw his arrow sticking out of the monster's front leg, as insignificant as a thistle. Then the monster stepped toward him. The ground trembled.

But the monster stopped. It cocked its head and made a sound. The sound was low and rumbly and had a question mark at the end. It sounded like, "How do you taste?"

Felix's legs felt like tree roots.

The monster took another step forward. Then it took a step back. It tilted its head the other way.

"Feeeeeliiiiiiix!" yelled Felix. "Help me!"

The monster's eyes grew wider. It opened its massive mouth and let loose a roar that filled the forest and echoed across the valley.

Felix turned and ran. Gripping his bow and arrows, he dodged tree trunks and leaped over fallen logs. He splashed through puddles and slipped in the mud.

The monster followed. Behind Felix, it sounded as though the forest itself were being uprooted. Trees cracked and broke and rocks clacked and tumbled. The ground shook and the monster bellowed and snarled. It was faster than it looked.

Felix, running too quickly to be careful, stepped on a flat, white mushroom as big as a dinner plate. There was a wet, tearing sound as his foot slipped and shot out from under him. He fell flat on his back. For a moment, he couldn't breathe. He had had the wind knocked right out of him.

He looked back. The monster was smashing through the trees. Its low, angry eyes were locked on him.

Felix climbed to his feet. His chest still felt empty. He took one tiny, limping step. Then another. His lungs working frantically, he finally drew a breath. He took another step. He breathed out, then in again. Then took another step.

The noise was so loud behind him that Felix was afraid to turn around. At any moment, he expected to be flattened by an armored hoof. But with each breath he drew, he went faster. His walking became a sort of skipping jog—and then, finally, he could run again.

The clearing was ahead, just past a thick stand of trees. At the center was a curious tree whose two trunks made a V. Felix ran straight for it. He timed his steps and leaped through the V. Then he was in the sunny meadow, running over clumpy hillocks of grass. He glanced back. The heavy timber had only slowed down the monster a little bit.

Then the Other Felix came running out of the woods. Felix's heart leaped. The Other Felix would fight the monster.

The monster burst into the clearing in an explosion of sticks and leaves. But the Other Felix wasn't running toward the monster. He was running full-tilt toward the tower, just like Felix.

Felix reached the tower door first. He kicked it open. He turned and watched as the monster gathered its legs and lowered its head. It sprang forward, coming halfway to the tower in one leap. The ground shook when it landed.

The Other Felix reached the tower. Both boys tumbled inside. Felix pushed the door shut with his shoulder. He lifted the heavy bolt and dropped it into place.

A moment later the earth thundered again. The monster had leaped again and had landed just outside the door. They heard it whuffing and felt the timbers groan as its massive head tested the door.

Then the monster seemed to walk away. As the two boys backed away from the door, Felix tripped over the cold stove. He stood up quickly, trying to get his breathing under control.

They felt the rumbling before they heard it. Then there was a thunderous bang and daylight flared around the corners of the door. The monster was trying to break it down.

The Other Felix stood in the center of the room, facing the door. Felix crept into the corner and crouched under the ladder.

The monster went away again. Then again there was a rumble as it ran forward. With a boom and a crack, the door gave way and flew across the room, where it knocked the stove over. Black soot puffed out of the broken chimney.

The monster's head came through the doorway. Its shoulders were blocked by the door frame. It looked right, then left, as if it couldn't see in the dim light. Then it saw the Other Felix. The monster's mouth opened and closed several times as if it was practicing eating him. Its hideous fat tongue slobbered drool onto the floor.

"Quick!" said the Other Felix. "Up the ladder!"

Felix climbed the ladder to the second floor, then the third. The Other Felix followed close behind. The monster's roars made the whole tower tremble. On the third floor, they looked out the window. The monster was walking backward, its six legs as thick as tree trunks. Then it ran forward, its head low, and crashed into the doorway like a battering ram. Both boys stumbled backward as the tower lurched. They looked out again. The monster's head was inside but it still couldn't get its shoulders past the door frame. It roared in rage and frustration.

"What's happening?" asked Felix. "Why don't you fight him?"

"I can't," said the Other Felix. "Something's wrong."

"If you don't fight him, he's going to knock the tower over."

"I know."

Felix looked at his friend and saw something that scared him even more than the monster did: the Other Felix was scared, too.

THIRTEEN

Felix went from window to window, watching as the monster circled the building, sniffing and pawing the logs. Every now and then it raised itself on its hind legs and peered into the second-story windows. It had stopped using its head as a battering ram, but each time it touched the wall, Felix could feel the whole tower shudder.

The monster was getting noisier, too, its bellows and cries like a weird form of speech. The sounds made Felix feel almost as frightened as the actual attacks on the tower. Without a moment of quiet, he couldn't even think. What were they going to do?

"I don't understand," said Felix. "Why can't you make him go away?"

"I don't know," said the Other Felix. "I always could before."

"Before what?"

"Before you came."

"You can't fight the monster because of me?"

"Things are changing now that you're here."

"I thought things were getting better."

"I thought so, too," said the Other Felix.

After a long time the monster grew quiet. Felix wondered if it was listening. He listened, too. Then he heard, from far away in the forest, a trumpeting call.

Another monster was answering.

The monster at the foot of the tower grunted. It sounded pleased.

"Oh, no," said the Other Felix.

Over the next hour, caws, howls, and shrieks came from all directions, as if every monster in the dreamland was coming to the tower. The monster below had stopped trying to get in, but Felix didn't feel any better. When the army of monsters finally arrived, the tower would be smashed to matchsticks.

The Other Felix climbed through the trapdoor onto the roof. Felix followed him. The wind was whipping around them and Felix had to hang on tight as he crawled to the center to sit down. The clouds were lowering and the sky was getting darker. Night was coming.

They saw trees swaying where monsters were coming through the woods. They heard the monsters' voices, a terrible choir, growing louder and louder. And, looking up, they saw a dark speck circling high above them.

"Flying monster," said the Other Felix. "We have to go back down."

Quickly, they slid across the roof, lowered themselves through the trapdoor, and closed it behind them.

They waited at the windows until they saw the dark and terrible shapes come out of the woods. The monsters began crossing the clearing.

Then Felix had an idea.

"I'm going to go to sleep," he said.

"What?" said the Other Felix.

"You said that things are changing because I'm here, and now you can't fight the monsters. If I leave, maybe you can fight them again."

"But what if I can't?"

"This isn't real, Felix," said Felix. "It's just a dream."

The Other Felix didn't say anything as Felix crept quietly down the ladder to the second floor. The dream day was almost done—if he went to sleep, he would wake up at home, in his own bed. With shaking hands, he changed out of the Other Felix's clothes and into his own pajamas. He lay down on one of the beds, put his head on the soft pillow, and pulled up the covers. He closed his eyes.

Outside, it sounded as if every creature had been let out of every zoo in the world. The noise was deafening.

Felix told himself to ignore it. He turned on his side and snuggled into the covers. He took a deep breath, then another. He made himself yawn.

He was wide awake.

Despite what he had told the Other Felix, the dreamland didn't feel like just a dream anymore. And when he disappeared back into the real world, the Other Felix would be alone again. Alone with the monsters. But it *was* only a dream.

If it's only a dream, wondered Felix, *then what am I so afraid of?*

He tried counting sheep, but just as each white, fluffy sheep leaped over the fence in his imagined pasture, it turned into a scaly monster and flapped away on black, leathery wings. Somewhere along the way he lost track of how many he had counted. Had he fallen asleep? Hoping very much to find himself back in his bed at home, he opened his eyes.

Other eyes were staring back at him. Eight glowing red eyes. Peering through the narrow window was a monster with a spider's head.

Felix screamed and picked up his bow. He knew it was useless but he wouldn't let the monsters win without a fight. He nocked an arrow, bent the bow, and shot at the ugly insect head. The arrow struck the monster right where its nose would have been, if it had had a nose. Even though it didn't have eyebrows, either, on its shiny brown head, it seemed to frown with all eight of its eyes.

Then it dropped out of sight.

There was a roar from below, as the other monsters saw it fall.

Felix nocked his last arrow and went to the window. *Maybe this isn't useless,* he thought. *Maybe if I shoot one more, I can scare them away.*

But what he saw scared him back into the room. There must have been three dozen monsters, of all shapes and sizes, on that side of the tower alone. Shooting an arrow at them would have been like trying to stop a fleet of city buses with a snowball. Defeated, he lowered the bow.

The Other Felix climbed down the ladder into the room. He gave Felix a downcast look and then climbed down to the first floor.

In a moment, Felix heard something over the monsters' hue and cry. A whistle. Then a shout. He ran to the window again and looked out.

The monsters had fallen quiet. They were all watching the tower doorway below.

"Go on, get!" shouted the Other Felix.

The Other Felix walked out of the tower, right up to the monsters. He was tiny compared with them. The monsters stayed quiet but didn't move. They simply watched and waited as the small boy walked steadily toward them.

The Other Felix kept walking. And, as he drew closer, some of them shook their heads and shied away. They snorted and whinnied.

But not the big, scaly, armor-plated monster that had started it all. It stood, unmoving, its massive head low to the ground—and aimed squarely at the Other Felix.

The Other Felix walked right up to the big monster. The big monster lifted a stumpy leg and knocked the Other Felix down. The other monsters began to crowd around.

Watching from the tower, Felix gasped. His friend was about to get eaten.

But the Other Felix sat up. Slowly, as if he was dizzy, he climbed to his feet. He approached the armor-plated monster again. This time, the monster didn't knock him down.

The Other Felix reached out and grabbed the monster's nose. He twisted it sideways, hard, and the monster, big as a city bus, yelped and skittered sideways, too, stepping on several other monsters as it did. One of the other monsters fell over.

Then the Other Felix picked up a baseball-sized rock and threw it. It flew flat and fast and hit a cow-sized monster in the eye. The cow-sized monster shrieked and galloped away.

The Other Felix strung his bow, nocked an arrow, and aimed it straight up into the sky. There was a *zing!* as the arrow flew up, and a *skrawk!* as it struck its target. Felix couldn't see the flying monster from his window, but he heard its wings flapping as it flew away.

There was a sudden stampede as every monster tried to escape from the Other Felix as fast as it could, not caring whether there was another monster in its way. It looked like a demolition derby as monsters crashed, fell, and stumbled to their feet before speeding haphazardly away.

A few minutes later, they were all gone.

Felix practically slid down the ladders. He reached the first floor just as the Other Felix was coming in. The Other Felix was muddy where he'd fallen, and his face was red from the monster's kick.

"You did it!" shouted Felix. "You chased them all away!"

He started crossing the room to give the Other Felix a grateful hug, but something in his friend's eyes made him stop.

"I did it this time. But I don't know if I can do it again. They're just not afraid of me anymore. I can tell."

Felix looked at the Other Felix's tired face. He thought of how much courage it had taken for the Other Felix to walk out to the monsters when he didn't know what would happen. He took a deep breath.

"Then show me how to fight the monsters," he said.

FOURTEEN

On the playground, the other kids told Felix, "Don't steal this soccer ball." In the lunchroom, they said, "Don't steal my cookie." In class, when Miss Olu's back was turned, they put their hands over their calculators, even if Felix was too far away to reach them. Even though he had his own calculator.

Chase didn't look even a little bit sorry. In fact, he laughed harder than everybody else.

Felix had asked his parents for help with his quandary, but they didn't seem to know what to do, either. How could it be all right to just let Chase do whatever he wanted? Felix needed to get back at Chase. To do that, he needed a plan.

He had seen a movie where a bad kid had taken the screws out of the teacher's chair. When the teacher sat down, the chair fell apart, and the teacher fell on the floor. Felix thought about taking the screws out of Miss Olu's chair and leaving the screwdriver in Chase's desk.

Then he pictured Miss Olu lying on the ground. He didn't want to hurt her. What he wanted was for the other kids to stop calling him a thief. He wanted Chase to know what it felt like to have everyone think he was a bad kid. And he wanted Miss Olu to be as disappointed in Chase as she was in Felix.

Felix watched Chase carefully. He noticed that Miss Olu often took extra time with Chase, talking to him or helping him find the right answer. Even though Chase was very confident, he often had a hard time getting answers right.

It seemed unfair that Miss Olu would spend more time with a boy like Chase, who wasn't very good at school, than with Felix, who worked hard and usually knew the right answer. Even when Chase gave a wrong answer or refused to answer, Miss Olu still smiled at him. Maybe not her biggest, best smile, the kind where her eyes crinkled up, but a smile all the same.

That made it even harder for Felix to make a

plan. If Miss Olu wasn't going to be upset with Chase when he did badly at school, how would anything make her upset with him?

Felix realized that he didn't know very much about Miss Olu. During class, she smiled and was cheerful and paid close attention to the students. He had never seen her outside the school. He had seen her before the school day started, talking on a pink cell phone with a little string of glittering diamonds hanging from it. The phone looked funny, like a doll's phone, and it played a song when it rang: "Over the Rainbow."

When the morning bell rang, Miss Olu always turned off her phone. She put the phone in her purse and put the purse in a drawer in her desk. But at lunchtime, and at the end of the day when the students were leaving, Miss Olu would take out her phone again.

Felix had heard one teacher say to another, "How can she afford to talk to Nigeria all the time like that?"

Miss Olu loved her family. Miss Olu loved her phone. Felix had an idea.

That night, Felix asked his mother how much a cell phone cost.

"It depends," she said. "Some phones cost hundreds of dollars, but some phones they give you for free when you sign a contract."

"What about a tiny pink phone?" Felix asked. "With diamonds on it?"

Felix's mother looked up from the TV and smiled. "Real diamonds or rhinestones?"

"I don't know."

"Are you thinking about buying one?"

"No," said Felix. "I'm just curious."

"You have an awfully specific curiosity."

"I just wondered if they were expensive."

She started watching TV again. "With diamonds on them, they sure would be. You should probably stick with the rhinestones. But what makes phones really precious to people is that they have all their numbers and appointments in them. It's a lot harder to replace those things than just a phone."

"Oh, okay," said Felix.

"Did you do your homework?" asked Felix's mother.

"Yes," said Felix.

"Then come over here and sit with me."

Felix sat down on the other end of the couch. His mother patted the middle cushion and smiled. He moved over. She kissed him on the top of his head. He leaned his head against her shoulder. She smelled like hospital soap. He didn't like the way the soap smelled but it had always made him feel better, simply because that was the way his mother smelled. Tonight it reminded him of all the kids at the hospital, kids whose problems could be figured out with stethoscopes and X-rays. The soap smell tickled his nose, but he didn't want to pull away from his mother, so he breathed through his mouth.

On the TV was a cooking show. Cooking was easy, thought Felix sleepily. The hard part was catching your own food.

FIFTEEN

Felix and the Other Felix walked down a path in the woods, going toward the pools where the monsters splashed and wallowed. Felix was excited to learn how to fight them. He was nervous, too. What if he couldn't do it? Though he had his bow slung over his back, Felix knew there was a secret that had nothing to do with weapons, something else that could make a big monster afraid of a small kid.

The Other Felix was in front. He started talking without turning around.

"Do you really want to fight the monsters, or do you just want to be able to get away from them?"

It was a good question. Felix thought hard before he answered.

"I guess I don't really want to fight them. But if I don't know how to fight them, what happens when I can't get away?"

"If you go to sleep, you'll go away and they won't be able to hurt you."

"I can't sleep when I'm scared," he said. "I tried that before, when the monsters were all around the tower."

"The book called *How to Sleep* has sleeping secrets," said the Other Felix. "I can teach them to you. Then you won't have to fight the monsters."

"They won't work. If a monster was chasing me, I wouldn't be able to fall asleep. Just like I couldn't fall asleep now, even if I wanted to."

The Other Felix stopped. He turned around. "Want to bet?"

"Bet what?" said Felix. "I don't have anything."

"A gentleman's bet," said the Other Felix. "That means you don't have to give me anything when you lose. But at least I'll know you'll know I'm right."

Felix agreed to the gentleman's bet. He knew he couldn't lose. The Other Felix couldn't make him fall asleep if he wasn't tired. Especially when the sun was high above them.

They walked off the trail to a large rock in the woods. Half of the rock was in sun and half of it was in shadow. They sat on the sunny side, resting their backs against it. Felix could feel a nighttime chill coming from deep inside the rock. But with the sun shining on his head, and bugs spinning lazily in shafts of light, Felix suddenly wondered if he wasn't sleepy, after all. He opened his eyes wide and swallowed a yawn.

"Okay," said the Other Felix. "Here's the secret. If you do it right, you'll fall asleep every time, I guarantee it."

"It better work fast," said Felix. "If a monster's running toward me, I won't have time to read myself a bedtime story."

"You won't have time to read anything. This works really fast. Ready?"

Felix nodded.

"Okay. Close your eyes and move your head in a circle. Counterclockwise. That means backward from the way a clock normally moves."

"I know that," said Felix.

"Now, with your eyes closed, and moving your head in a circle—slowly—count from twelve down to one. After every number, say, 'I can't go to sleep.'"

"That's stupid," said Felix. "That will never work."

"Then you'll win the bet. Are you going to try it or not?"

Felix sighed. He closed his eyes. He started

moving his head in a counterclockwise circle. "Twelve. I can't go to sleep. Eleven. I can't go to sleep. Ten. I can't go to sleep. Nine. This will never work."

"You have to do it right or the bet's off," said the Other Felix.

"Nine. I can't go to sleep. Eight. I can't go to sleep. Seven. I can't go to sleep."

Felix yawned.

"Six. I can't go to sleep. Five. I can't go to sleep. Four—"

SIXTEEN

Felix woke up. He was confused. Only a moment ago, he had been leaning against a warm rock in a clearing in the forest. Now he was in his bedroom. The covers were piled up, making him feel as if he were in a nest. He was sweaty and hot. He was still wearing the Other Felix's flannel shirt and corduroy pants.

He threw off the covers. He looked at the clock. It showed just after three in the morning.

Felix didn't want to be awake. He wanted to learn how to fight monsters. But now, not only was he awake, he was wide awake.

He lay there, watching the glowing numbers on

the clock. They counted off thirty minutes and he still wasn't the least bit sleepy.

Suddenly, he laughed. Then he sat up in bed. He closed his eyes. He began moving his head in a counterclockwise circle.

"Twelve," he said. "I can't go to sleep."

SEVENTEEN

He woke up. He was sitting with his back against the rock. The sun was falling behind the tree-tops. He stood up and looked around.

The Other Felix was gone.

Felix walked to the trail. He wished the Other Felix hadn't gone on without him. He didn't want to see any monsters until he had learned how to fight them.

"Of course," he said to himself, "if I see a monster, I can always go to sleep."

He paused.

"If it's not running too fast," he added.

Hesitantly, he continued on toward the pools. The trees cast long shadows across the trail. The insects had stopped buzzing. Every now and then a bird tweeted without hearing an answer. The trail climbed and the air grew cooler. Then, finally, puffs of steam drifted out of the trees and Felix knew he had arrived.

Picking his way through big, muddy footprints, he climbed the last little way. The Other Felix was sitting with his back to the trail, soaking his bare feet in a hot pool.

"I win the bet," said the Other Felix.

"What happens when I fall asleep?" asked Felix.

"When you fall asleep here? You go away."

"I just . . . vanish?"

"It's more like a flicker. Like a candle when you blow on it. And then you're gone."

"Is there smoke?"

The Other Felix laughed, a little meanly, Felix thought. "No, there's no *smoke*."

Felix sat down by the pool. He took off his borrowed shoes and rolled up his pant legs. He dipped a toe in the water, yelped, and pulled it out. Then, slowly, he put his toe back in. After a few minutes he was able to put in his whole foot. Then his other foot. After a while, the heat stopped hurting and took away the soreness from the long walk up the trail.

"I still want you to teach me how to fight the monsters," said Felix.

"I know," said the Other Felix.

"I mean, I don't want to have to fight them, ever. But I don't want to have to run away all the time, either. And if I can't fight them, and you can't fight them, I don't want to come here anymore."

The Other Felix stared at the rippling sheets of steam that rose off the quiet pool.

"I know," he said.

Felix looked around. The other time they had come to the pools, he had been too frightened to really see his surroundings. He had noticed the damp clumps of fur clinging to the thornbushes, the slick rocks, and the mud. But he hadn't noticed how high the cliffs rose and how cold the rocks were. He hadn't seen the muddy, heavily used paths that wound around the pools and then disappeared into a great cleft in the cliff face.

Felix heard a shuddering moan, just at the edge of hearing, echo out of the cleft.

"Why did we come here?" he asked.

The Other Felix finally lifted his head and looked Felix in the eye. "Because there are always monsters around here."

Wood cracked in the forest. Rocks clattered in the canyon.

"This is where they live," said the Other Felix.

Just then, a large bush began to shake, its branches

whipping the air and throwing off fat drops of mud. Then the bush rose up and, with it, roots and dirt and rocks. Among the rocks were two coal-black eyes and a row of glittering teeth. The monster rose out of a steaming pool, growing taller and taller until its shadow covered them like night. It opened its mouth with a sound of grinding rocks. Then it roared. Its roar sounded like explosions going off deep underground—and getting closer and closer to the surface. The noise was deafening.

Felix stood up and jumped back. He slipped and fell in the mud. The monster's massive head swung down with astonishing quickness, and its dull black eyes looked directly into his own.

"How do you fight a monster like this?" yelled Felix.

"The same way you fight any monster," said the Other Felix. "Even a little one."

The monster's legs were great columns of rock. It took one step forward—and stopped. Its giant foot was just across the pool from the Other Felix. If it took one more step, the Other Felix would be crushed into the steaming pool of hot water and drowned.

Terrified, Felix began crawling backward in the mud.

But the Other Felix didn't move. The monster's

109

head tilted, and small stones broke loose and rained into the water, splashing the Other Felix.

"They're too big," said the Other Felix. "If you only fight them with your hands, or with arrows and rocks, you can't win. But you have something that makes you more powerful than they are."

Craning his neck up at the rock monster towering over them, Felix could not imagine anything that would make him feel more powerful than it.

And yet, though the monster could have crushed the Other Felix simply by taking one more step, it didn't take that step.

"Come here, Felix," said the Other Felix.

Felix stood up, the mud cooling on his skin. He wanted to turn around and run the other way.

"Come here."

Too frightened to breathe, Felix took one step forward, then another, and another, until he was standing beside the Other Felix at the monster's foot. It felt like standing at the foot of an apartment building—a building that was about to fall on him.

"Happiness is more powerful than unhappiness," said the Other Felix. "Do you think the monsters are happy here?"

Felix looked around at the cold rocks and sharp thorns.

"No," he said.

"You can leave," said the Other Felix. "But they live here. We live here."

Felix took a few steps back. He wasn't running away this time, only trying to get a better look at the monster's eyes. The eyes were black, with no irises or pupils, and Felix didn't think he saw anything there. But, suddenly, he felt something: he felt the sadness of living in a dark cave in a lonely land, of being ugly and huge and clumsy. Of speaking a language that no one could understand. Of inspiring fear, not love.

And he felt the monster's terrible anger at the kid in front of him—a kid with the courage to simply stand and look.

"Go away," whispered Felix. "Go away."

The monster shifted its weight but stood still.

"Go away," said Felix, more loudly.

The monster took one crunching step backward and stopped.

"Sometimes it helps to throw things," said the Other Felix. "Just to show them who's boss."

Felix lifted a stone out of the mud, a stone that had fallen off the monster itself. He threw it as high and hard as he could.

"Go away!" he shouted. "Go on, go home!"

The stone struck the monster in its bulging stomach. It bounced harmlessly away. But the monster took two more backward steps, then two more, then turned and began thundering away.

Felix jumped up and down, his feet squelching in the muck at the edge of the pool. "Go on! Go! Get out of here!"

The monster's mighty foot splashed into a deep pool, making it erupt in a cloud of hissing steam. Its other foot struck a pine tree, bending it until it cracked with a sound like a cannon, the yellow wood inside it exploding into jagged splinters. The ground quaked as the monster climbed the trail to the cleft in the cliff wall and disappeared. For a while they heard sounds like thunder in a passing storm. Then, finally, it grew quiet.

Overjoyed, thrilled at his power, Felix shouted to the sky. "That . . . was . . . incredible!"

But the Other Felix didn't join his celebration, didn't high-five him or even grin. Instead, he stood up, turned, and started down the trail in his wet bare feet, holding his shoes.

Puzzled, Felix followed him.

EIGHTEEN

Felix ate his cereal and watched the rain. Thin streaks of water dripped slowly down the glass. When two streaks met, they flowed faster. Once in a while, a gust of wind made the window shudder and a burst of raindrops would spatter the pane as if they had been spat on it.

By a monster. Only a monster would have been able to spit so high.

Felix looked down at his bowl. Three soggy flakes of cereal were drowning in a lake of milk. He shook more cereal into the bowl and stirred until each dry flake had been dunked. He looked longingly at the sugar, high on a kitchen shelf. His mother said there was enough sugar in the cereal already. Felix disagreed.

His mother came down the hallway, leaning back to balance the heavy basket of laundry she was holding.

"Did you go to sleep wearing your shoes, Felix?" she asked angrily.

Felix looked down at his feet. Ever since his mother had gotten him a new pair of slippers, he was careful not to wear his own slippers or shoes to the dreamland. He borrowed the Other Felix's shoes instead. And he was careful to leave the Other Felix's shoes in the dreamland. But he had been wearing them last night, when the Other Felix had taught him the secret of falling asleep.

"No," he said, truthfully. "I didn't go to sleep wearing my shoes."

Felix's mother closed her eyes and let her breath out slowly. She shook her head. Then she went back down the hall. Felix heard her throw open the washing-machine door.

"Mud!" she muttered. "On his sheets!"

After breakfast, Felix put his homework in his backpack. He put on his rain boots and his raincoat and pulled up the hood. His mother, putting on an earring, bent down to kiss him before he went out the door. The door swung shut and locked behind him.

He had to wait a long time before he could get on the elevator. Then the doors opened on the floor below and Mrs. Nowak got on wearing her raincoat and galoshes and towing her folded grocery cart.

"Good morning, Felix," said Mrs. Nowak, as the doors closed.

"Good morning, Mrs. Nowak," said Felix.

"It's an ugly day out there. It's a shame we have to go out, isn't it?"

"Why don't you shop at the little store?" he asked, puzzled. There was a small grocery store on the first floor of the building whose sign read, EVERYTHING YOU HAVE TO HAVE.

"Too expensive!" said Mrs. Nowak. "And they don't have pickled herring or my magazines."

Felix had watched Mrs. Nowak eat gray, slimy pickled herring. He thought that, if he were ever stranded in the dreamland with nothing to eat but pickled herring, he would rather starve.

On the sidewalk, Felix watched Mrs. Nowak hunch against the wind and rain and walk slowly away. He walked to the crosswalk. The crossing guard wasn't there. He pushed the button to cross and waited for the light to change. He counted cars and reached forty-one before the orange hand changed to a white person. He looked both ways to make sure the cars were stopped and then stepped off the curb.

A hand grabbed his arm. Startled, he looked up. A gray-haired old man in a wet wool shirt was holding him firmly.

"Gotta be careful on the big streets, sonny," said the old man.

The man marched him across the street. He held Felix's arm too tightly and pulled too hard, but he let go as soon as they reached the sidewalk.

"There you go," he said.

Felix stood there, rubbing his arm. His mother would have expected him to say "Thank you," but he didn't like being treated like a little kid.

"You tell your mom to tell you to be careful," said the old man.

The old man turned away and, sheltering his mouth with his hands, lit a cigarette. As soon as he lowered his hands, the rain made the cigarette fall apart. Shaking his head and muttering, the old man walked off down the street with flecks of wet paper and tobacco stuck to his chin.

Felix punched his fist into his open palm, but it didn't make him feel any tougher.

•   •   •

Felix said good morning to the guard and went up-stairs. When he reached the second floor, he saw Miss Olu coming toward him, talking happily on her phone. He reached the room before she did and went in. He took off his backpack and his coat. He hung his coat on his peg and pretended to look at something on the bulletin board when Miss Olu came through the door. She was just finishing her conversation. Felix watched her out of the corner of his eye as she turned the phone off and put it in her purse. She put her purse in the bottom right drawer of her desk and closed it. She took off her coat.

"Good morning, Felix!" she said.

"Good morning," said Felix.

"What, don't you have a smile for me today?"

Felix smiled, but it felt funny because he didn't mean it.

Throughout the day, Felix watched carefully for his chance to take the phone. But at lunch, Miss Olu took her purse with her. She kept it looped over her shoulder while she got her food and put it next to her tray while she ate. At recess, it was Felix's turn to be line leader and so he couldn't wait behind. By the end of the day, he was convinced that it would be impossible to take Miss Olu's phone. He didn't use the word *steal* when he thought about it because he knew she would get the phone back in the end.

Then, at the end of the day, he saw his chance. The bell had rung and there were only a few students left in the room: Marina, Jasper, Chase, and Felix. Miss Olu was helping Marina solve a problem. Jasper and Chase had been asked to wipe off the whiteboards. And Felix was just waiting around.

Then, Marina thanked Miss Olu and went to get her coat and backpack. Miss Olu sat down at her desk, took her purse out of the drawer, and took her phone out of the purse. The phone beeped as she turned it on.

Mr. Savage, the principal, stuck his head through the door.

"Ah, you're still here," he said to Miss Olu. "A quick word?"

Miss Olu smiled and nodded. She set her phone down on the desk and followed Mr. Savage out into the hall. The door closed.

Chase and Jasper finished wiping the whiteboards and threw the erasers at each other. Then they picked up the erasers, put them away, and left.

Felix took a deep breath and ran up to the front of the room. He was so scared he felt as though he could hardly see. He grabbed Miss Olu's phone and ran back to Chase's desk. He lifted the top of the desk. Inside was a mess of chewed pencils with chewed erasers and crumpled pieces of paper. Felix pushed the phone down to the bottom and closed the desk. He looked at the door, expecting it to open at any moment. It didn't open.

Half a minute later, Felix was wearing his coat and backpack and pushing through the door into the hall. He expected to see Miss Olu and Mr. Savage standing in the hall but neither of them was there. He closed the door, walked down the hall, and went downstairs.

When he opened the front door, rain spat in his face. He pulled up his hood and went to cross the street. The crossing guard was there this time.

NINETEEN

That night, Felix found it hard to sleep. His mind raced as he imagined what would happen the next day at school. Even if no one had seen him take Miss Olu's phone and hide it in Chase's desk, he half expected Miss Olu to guess the truth just by looking at him. How had Chase sounded so honest when he lied about Felix? Felix was growing increasingly certain that he would confess everything the moment Miss Olu walked in the door.

Finally, by sitting up in bed and doing the falling-asleep trick, he was able to escape into the dreamland.

As usual, when he woke up on the second floor of the wooden tower, he changed out of his pajamas and slippers and into the Other Felix's clothes. Hearing the Other Felix moving around down-stairs, he hurried down the ladder.

The Other Felix was wearing a jacket and boots. He had a backpack on his back and a canteen slung over his shoulder. He was just taking his bow and arrows down from the wall.

"Where are we going?" asked Felix happily. "Hunting?"

"*I* am going camping," said the Other Felix.

"Can I come, too?"

The Other Felix opened the door and went out-side. Felix followed him.

"Why do you want to come? You don't need me to fight monsters anymore."

"I want to go because I think it would be fun. It's lonely being here by myself."

"All right," said the Other Felix grumpily. "Hurry and get your stuff."

The Other Felix started walking slowly toward the trees. Felix hurried back to the tower to get his bow and arrows. By the time he got back out, the Other Felix was almost to the woods. Felix ran hard, but by the time he reached the trees, the Other Felix was nowhere to be seen. Felix hurried down the trail. He wondered why the Other Felix was acting so strangely.

Finally, he caught up. The Other Felix was striding briskly up the trail. He didn't look back. But Felix felt more content. The Other Felix was just in a bad mood. Maybe he would find an animal to hunt and then he would feel better.

As they walked, Felix watched the forest. He remembered the giant rock monster's retreat and felt a surge of excitement. He felt powerful. If he could fight monsters, just like the Other Felix could, then he had nothing to be afraid of.

Maybe he could even fight monsters better than the Other Felix. Maybe that was why the Other Felix was in such a bad mood.

"Are you thinking about the monsters?" said the Other Felix suddenly.

"Yes," said Felix.

"You probably think it's easy. It's easy if someone shows you how to do it. But sometimes things are . . . different. Different monsters do different things. And then it can be hard again."

"Why are you telling me this? I did a good job."

"That was only one monster," said the Other Felix.

"It was the biggest monster I've ever seen," mumbled Felix.

"What did you say?" asked the Other Felix sharply.

"Nothing."

As they walked on up the trail, Felix began to wish he hadn't begged to come along. The camping trip wasn't much fun. But now he didn't want to turn back alone. What if there was more to fighting monsters than he knew about?

Suddenly, the Other Felix stopped. He raised his hand. Felix stopped, too. They listened. The Other Felix fitted an arrow to his bow. He began to turn, scanning the forest canopy above them.

Felix looked and listened but didn't see or hear anything. The Other Felix kept turning until he was facing back down the trail, toward Felix. Suddenly, he raised his bow and pulled the string taut—with the arrow pointed right at Felix's head.

Felix ducked. He heard the *strum!* of the bowstring and the *thwip!* of the arrow as it sailed overhead. Sitting on his bottom on the trail, he watched the arrow's flight. It struck a tree with a *knock!* and quivered gently. From the branch above, a bird flapped furiously into the leaves and disappeared.

"You could have hit me!" said Felix, astonished.

"Good thing you ducked," said the Other Felix.

When darkness fell, they made a fire right in the middle of the trail. They laid blankets on either side and sat on them. They ate sandwiches and chips and drank bottles of cold root beer that the Other Felix took out of his pack.

"Do you have a forest where you live?" asked the Other Felix suddenly.

"No," said Felix. "We have parks and play-grounds, though."

"How many friends do you have there?"

"None, really. But I get to play with a bunch of kids at school."

"And your mom makes all your food for you?"

"Except when I'm at school. Then the lunch lady makes it."

The Other Felix stirred the fire. Wood popped and orange sparks flew upward in the dark night.

"Do you think you could take me with you sometime?"

Felix laughed. "I'm only dreaming you. I can't take you with me, Felix."

"Maybe this is real life and you're only dream-ing your home. Or maybe this is all *my* dream."

"Have you ever gone anywhere else when you sleep?" asked Felix.

The Other Felix shook his head sadly. "No."

The fire burned down to embers. After a while they lay down on their blankets and watched the stars wink through dark tree branches.

"Someday you'll stop coming," said the Other Felix quietly. "And I'll be alone again."

Felix wanted to tell him no, that he would always come. But, in his heart, he wondered if the Other Felix was right. And, anyway, he couldn't control his dreams, could he?

TWENTY

It was a dark morning. It was still raining. The lights of passing cars made white and red smudges on the wet street as Felix waited at the crosswalk, across from the crossing guard. When an angry driver passed a too-slow car, its wheels splashed water out of a pothole onto Felix's boots.

Then the light changed. The crossing guard stepped out, raised her red stop sign, and cautioned the slowing cars with the palm of her hand. The cars stopped. Felix crossed the street.

On the other side, he looked up, blinking against the raindrops. A car had pulled to the curb and its door was opening. A kid was getting out. That was against the rules: because of the heavy traffic, all drop-offs were supposed to take place in the parking lot behind the school.

Chase got out of the car. He was wearing a light jacket and no hat. His brown hair was already wet. His father was shouting at him.

"It's not my job to hold your hand while you get ready in the morning! The alarm goes off, you get up! You get dressed, you eat your breakfast! Brush your teeth and be ready when I'm ready to drive you to school! What part of that don't you understand, Chase? Chase? Look at me!"

Chase, who had been looking away, turned his head toward the car. But his eyes were low.

"And if your mom needs help, you help her! You know she's sad. She can't do everything she wants to do. And when you don't help, it only makes her sadder!"

Felix felt funny. He knew he was seeing something that he wasn't supposed to see, but he couldn't stop watching. Without thinking, he began walking slowly toward the car. He was halfway there when the crossing guard rushed past him, her yellow-green vest like a flash of lightning.

She stopped behind Chase and leaned down so she could see into the car. "Sir!" she said. "You're not allowed to let your child off here."

"What are you, a cop?" said Chase's father.

"It's not safe. There's too much traffic."

"Well, what do you want me to do about it now?"

"I want you to put your child in the car, buckle his seat belt, and drive around to the back of the school."

"You want me to what?"

"So you'll know the proper way to do it tomorrow."

"Listen, lady, if you're gonna write me a ticket, write me a ticket. Otherwise, we're done here."

The crossing guard glared angrily, but she didn't move. Even Felix knew that crossing guards couldn't write tickets.

Chase's father reached across the passenger seat and pulled the door closed. The car's wheels spun and the car lurched into traffic. Tires skidded and horns honked. Halfway down the block, Chase's dad's car slowed to a crawl in a crowd of cars.

The crossing guard stared after him, her mouth shut tight. Felix looked at Chase. Chase looked at Felix and then, ignoring him, walked toward the front door of the school. Chase's hair was as wet as if he had just taken a bath. Rain pattered on the hood of Felix's raincoat.

Felix thought of Miss Olu's phone, hidden in

Chase's desk. He decided to take it out. Chase was having a bad day already.

He started running. His boots splashed in a puddle. His socks got wet.

"Don't run!" called the crossing guard. "It's slippery!"

Chase had gone inside before Felix even started up the steps. Felix climbed the steps as fast as he could and pulled the heavy metal door open with both hands. He saw wet footprints crossing the green tile floor and climbing the stairs. He didn't see Chase.

Felix panted hello to the security guard and began running up the stairs.

"Slow down!" said the security guard. "Those stairs are wet!"

Felix didn't slow down. He ran up the first flight of stairs, holding on to the rail as his feet flew around the landing and up the second flight of stairs. When he reached the top, he saw the door to the classroom closing.

He ran to the door and opened it. Chase's jacket was on its peg. Felix whirled around. Chase was already at his desk, his head down on his arms as if he were sleeping.

Breathing hard, Felix shrugged off his backpack

and dropped it on the floor. He took off his raincoat and hung it up. Then he hung the backpack on top of the raincoat. He sat on the bench and took off his wet boots, then put his dry shoes on over his wet socks.

He went to his desk. Chase's head was turned toward the window. Water had dripped out of his hair and pooled on the desk. Felix pictured the little pink phone inside the desk.

"Chase," he said hesitantly.

Chase didn't move.

The door to the hall opened and Miss Olu came in, followed by several kids. She sat down at her desk.

Felix sat down. He looked at the clock. More kids came in. The bell rang and the kids quieted down. Miss Olu stood up and smiled at them.

"Good morning, children," she said. "Another wet day. Soon that rain will turn into snow and, believe it or not, we will miss the rain. Did you know that, where I grew up, I never saw even one snowflake? The first time I saw snow was the first day I came to this country. I walked out of the airport wearing only a light dress and I had no hat and no mittens. The temperature was ten degrees, the wind was blowing, and the ground was covered with something white that I had seen only in storybooks."

Felix liked the sound of Miss Olu's voice. She said her words carefully and there was something musical about the way she said them. It was as if, behind the words, a song was waiting to get out. Most of all, he liked the stories she told. Miss Olu's home reminded him of the pictures in Mrs. Nowak's books. But Miss Olu had seen those places with her own eyes. Those places were real.

"I am happy here, in this country, and especially with you, my dears. But I miss my home, sometimes. You have seen me talking on my little pink phone, I know. You probably think that I spend all my time talking on it! I am talking to my family and friends back home. Unfortunately, this morning I could not call my mother and talk to her. I lost my phone! I am absentminded sometimes, so I am sure that I set it down and walked away and forgot it. I have never lost my phone before, but I am sure that this is what happened."

Miss Olu smiled warmly. She crossed to the windows and began raising the half-closed shades until they were all the way open.

"Have any of you seen my phone? When I woke up this morning I had a happy thought, that one of you children had found my phone, and had put it in your pocket, and wanted to surprise me with what you had found."

Miss Olu raised another shade. The gray day began to seem less dark. Felix wished desperately that he had put the phone anywhere but the place he had put it. Chase's head was still down on his desk.

After raising all the shades, Miss Olu turned and leaned against the windowsill. Still smiling her warm smile, she called on several students by name.

"Jasper, have you seen my phone? Archie, have you seen it?"

Both kids shook their heads.

"Felix?"

Felix shook his head, too.

Miss Olu suddenly seemed to notice Chase.

"Chase, dear," she said, "are you ill?"

Chase didn't move. Miss Olu walked closer. She bent over Chase and put her hand on his back.

"Chase?"

Then, suddenly, a song began to play: "Over the Rainbow." And it wasn't just the notes of the song, the way many phones rang. It was a woman's voice, singing.

Somewhere, over the rainbow
Way up high
There's a land that I heard of
Once in a lullaby

Chase lifted his head. He stared at his desk. Miss Olu lifted the top of Chase's desk and gently moved things aside until she found her phone. She looked at the little screen on it and her smile returned.

"My mother," she said.

She pressed a button and the music stopped.

"There is no talking on phones during class, of course. I will have to call her back. Chase, would you come with me, please?"

Chase didn't move. "I didn't do it," he said.

Miss Olu's voice was warm but her hand on Chase's shoulder looked firm. "Chase. Come with me, please."

Chase stood up. His face was still wet from the rain. "I didn't do it," he said. But he followed Miss Olu into the hall.

Felix put his head down on his desk.

TWENTY-ONE

Felix woke up beside the trail. The blanket had fallen off during the night and he was shivering. The campfire had burned down to charred black sticks and wispy white ashes. Gray dawn was breaking. The Other Felix was gone.

The Other Felix's things were gone, too. Felix stood up, wrapping the blanket around his shoulders like a robe. He opened his backpack, hoping to find some food. There wasn't any. The Other Felix had been carrying the food.

"But if this is a dream," said Felix, thinking aloud, "I shouldn't need to eat."

And indeed he stopped feeling hungry.

"And if this is a dream," he added, "I shouldn't feel cold, either."

He still felt cold.

Felix took off the blanket and put on his backpack. Then he put the blanket on again and lifted the ends so they wouldn't trail on the ground. He picked up his bow and arrows and set off down the trail.

He had questions: Why was the Other Felix avoiding him? Weren't they friends? But, since the Other Felix wasn't around to answer his questions, Felix decided that he would just look for an adventure by himself.

The trail led him in a new direction, neither toward the stone steps nor toward the monsters' home. As it neared the valley wall, the trail curved and began descending into a hidden canyon. After a while, the canyon opened up into another valley, its broad slopes thick with green pine trees. Warmer now, Felix rested on a fallen log. He took off the blanket, folded it, and put it in his backpack.

He needed to pee. His mother had told him never to pee in a dream because, if he did, he would wet the bed in real life. But his mother had no idea how much time he spent in dreams.

"This is a dream," he said hopefully. "I shouldn't need to pee in a dream."

But he did need to pee. Badly. He looked up and down the trail. No one was coming, of course. Still, it seemed like bad manners to pee on the trail. So he walked into the woods.

He took twenty steps and stopped. He was completely walled in by trees. Setting his bow on the ground, he pulled down the front of his pajamas.

A branch snapped. Then another. There was a whispery sound that went from right to left. Then silence.

Felix listened, his head cocked.

He thought he heard footsteps. Was the Other Felix coming?

Suddenly, a monster the size of a mail truck burst out of the trees, dirt and pine needles flying behind it like the tail of a comet. The monster saw Felix and, digging its stumpy front legs into the ground, slid to a noisy halt. By the time it stopped, its nose was no more than a yard away from Felix's.

This monster's massive head was dish-shaped and armor-plated, like a dinosaur's. Broad horns stuck out to the left and right above its ears. Its mouth was like a bird's beak. It could have snapped Felix in two as easily as Felix would have broken a graham cracker.

The monster looked at Felix, its eyes wild. Its snorting breath was hot and damp on his face.

Then, just as suddenly as it had appeared, the monster reared up, twisted to one side, and galloped off. Behind it, broken trees and bushes made a new road through the woods.

Felix didn't have to pee anymore. He pulled up his pajamas.

"They really are afraid of me," he said, wonderingly.

Bending down to pick up his bow, Felix saw that it was broken. The monster had stepped on it. The arrows were broken, too. Tears welled up in the corners of his eyes. He had worked so hard making them. But he had never learned to shoot them right anyway. Maybe he didn't need them, after all. He left them lying on the ground. He wiped his eyes with the back of his hand.

Then he started following the monster.

After a while there were fewer fallen trees and broken bushes, as if the monster had slowed down and begun to walk more carefully. Soon it became difficult to follow the monster's path at all. Felix walked slowly, watching the ground for footprints and the trees for broken bark.

He heard a deep groan from somewhere in the woods.

Then he heard the Other Felix shout: "Monster . . . Monster!"

"Felix!" Felix shouted. "I'm over here!"

He listened, but there was no reply. Maybe the Other Felix was too far away to hear him.

He picked his way up a hillside covered with tussocks of green moss. He climbed over a fallen tree trunk. He crossed a perfect circle of tiny white mushrooms. And when he reached the top of the small hill, he realized that he had lost the monster's trail completely.

"Felix!" he shouted. "Felix!"

He listened. He heard the wind keening quietly in the trees, and nothing else. But he felt something. It was a feeling Felix had never had before, the feeling of knowing something without seeing, hearing, or smelling it. He knew where the monster was.

Felix looked down. The other side of the hill fell away quickly. It was too steep to climb down. He turned to his right and picked his way down, then began circling the base of the hill to the other side.

Halfway there he heard a snort, followed by a high, throaty cry that made his hair stand on end. He kept going, more slowly than before.

Then he saw the other side of the hill. He hadn't been able to climb down it because there was no other side. Some long-vanished river had carved it into a big, shallow cave. Dark shadows made it difficult for Felix to see inside.

But slowly his eyes adjusted. He saw a shape, then a jumble of shapes. Boulders, he thought. Then he realized that one of the boulders was the monster he had been following. Its gray armored hide was the perfect camouflage for its hiding place.

The monster was holding very still, but after a while Felix could see its side rise and fall as it breathed in and out. He could see the monster's eyes, watching him carefully.

It was afraid.

Felix took one step forward. The monster shrank back. The whole cave shrank back. Felix saw that the other boulders were monsters, too. It was a whole cave full of monsters—all of them lying still, and all of them watching him.

Felix felt cold fear in the pit of his stomach. He felt a sudden urge to flee. But if he did, then they would know that he was, after everything, still afraid of them. And if he was still afraid of them, they wouldn't be afraid of him.

He stood his ground. Then he took a deep breath. He took one more step.

The mass of monsters shrank back again. Because they were all huddled tightly together, it was difficult to tell how many of them there were. It wasn't even easy to tell where one monster ended and another one began. They crouched hoof to jowl, cheek to flank. One monster's head peered over another monster's back. There were all kinds of monsters. There were even, he saw, as he craned his neck and peered upward, flying monsters, hanging from the ceiling like bats.

They were all there, every monster he had ever seen in the dreamland—and some he hadn't— hiding in the cave.

The monsters were getting restless. They squirmed and fidgeted. They whimpered, moaned, and rumbled. Pressed as far as they could against the back of the cave, they couldn't retreat any farther. But with each step forward, Felix was making them more frightened. And the only way they could get out would be past Felix—or over the top of him.

Felix held up his hands. That frightened them, too. There was a panic that only quieted when he didn't move again.

"It's okay," said Felix. "I won't hurt you."

The monsters trembled.

"I really won't," said Felix.

Carefully, he picked his way up the rocky slope. He could feel their fear almost as if it were his own. The nearest monster, which looked something like a mangy lion, was cowering, its eyes rolled back into its head. Felix patted its paw reassuringly. He reached his fingers under its ruff and scratched its back. He felt ticks and burrs and dirty fur. He kept scratching. He felt the monster relax.

The other monsters began to relax, too. Felix climbed up among them, and on them, right to the center of the cave. Sitting on the back of the mail-truck-sized monster, he leaned against another monster's matted side.

The monsters looked different. Where before he had seen jagged claws and sharp teeth, he now saw watery eyes and slobbery tongues. Where he had seen hard scales and armored hides, he saw patchy fur and broken antlers. The Other Felix was right: the monsters really were unhappy.

Where before he had heard terrifying roars, now he heard—as he scratched the monster between two armored plates—purring.

Then he heard something else. A familiar voice calling from outside the cave.

"Here, monster, monster, monster," called the Other Felix. "Here, monster, monster, monster. Come on, monster, come to Felix."

Instantly, the monsters stiffened and grew silent.

"Here, monster. Come on, monster."

A great yellow eye unlidded itself, blinked, and stared at Felix. Felix understood: the monster was

141

confused. If Felix was here, inside the cave, how could he be outside the cave, too? If Felix was being kind to them, how could he be hunting them, too?

Because that's what the Other Felix was doing: he was hunting the monsters. They had been hiding from him.

The Other Felix was getting closer. He called the monsters as if he were calling kittens.

Then, as if pulled by a string, an arrow flew into the cave. It struck a monster in the leg. The big monster yelped, then cowered, whimpering.

Felix climbed down to the front of the cave. The Other Felix was just coming out of the trees. The Other Felix looked surprised to see him.

"I thought the monsters weren't afraid of you anymore," said Felix.

"They're not," said the Other Felix. "I was pretending to be you. What are you doing here?"

"I was trying to make them feel better."

"Are you friends with them now?"

"I don't know. But I don't think we have to be afraid of them anymore."

"That's easy for you to say."

"Why are you hunting them?" asked Felix.

"Because I hate them!" said the Other Felix.

The Other Felix shot another arrow into the cave. There was a cry as another monster was hit.

There were so many monsters and they were all so huge. If they wanted to, they could have crushed both Felixes. Like tanker ships sailing over two sand flies, they wouldn't have felt a bump. But they cowered in the cave, squirming and shrinking back.

Felix tried to count the arrows in the Other Felix's quiver. There might have been as many as a dozen.

"Don't you think that hurts them?" asked Felix.

"Of course it hurts them," said the Other Felix. "I want to hurt them. Don't you think they wanted to hurt me, all those times? Don't you think they wanted to hurt you?"

"They don't want to hurt me now."

"That's because they're afraid of you now."

Felix looked at the shaggy, scaly, and plated beasts he'd been sitting with only moments before. He had felt their contentment. He had even heard a monster purr! He couldn't believe it was only because they were afraid of him.

"No," he said. "No, they're not afraid of me now."

"They're only being nice because they're afraid of you," said the Other Felix.

"Stop it," said Felix. "Stop hunting them."

The Other Felix smiled. His smile was strange. Felix hadn't looked in a mirror lately, but he decided that the Other Felix didn't really look all that much like him, after all.

The Other Felix raised his bow. He pointed an arrow right at Felix.

"Then I'll hunt you," he said. "I'll catch you, and I'll make you stay here, too."

Felix jumped out of the way. He heard the arrow *zizz!* past and *thunk!* into something behind him. A monster bleated but Felix didn't have time to look back. He scrambled down the slope. He fell, rolled, and came up on his feet. He started running. He had almost reached the trees when an arrow struck a trunk next to him and splintered.

What happens if I die in my dream? wondered Felix. He didn't want to find out.

He heard the Other Felix running after him. The monsters would be able to sneak away.

"I'll get you!" shouted the Other Felix.

Felix dodged around tree trunks and leaped over rocks. He changed direction suddenly and without warning. He felt strong and fast. It was as if his feet were barely touching the ground.

He ran and ran until he couldn't run anymore. Gulping air, his chest heaving, he fell to his knees in a clearing. He couldn't see or hear the Other Felix.

Ahead of him was a thornbush as big as a small

house. The thorns, however, didn't go all the way to the ground. Lying on his stomach, Felix wriggled underneath, all the way to the center of the bush. Inside, next to the gnarled, twisted trunk, was a hollow space, like a little room, with a dry dirt floor. He couldn't see out of the bush and, he was sure, the Other Felix couldn't see in.

He wanted to go home.

Sitting down, he closed his eyes. He began moving his head in a counterclockwise circle.

"Twelve," he said. "I can't go to sleep."

And, just like that, he fell asleep.

TWENTY-TWO

Felix woke up. Drowsily, he rolled over and reached for his pillow. He pricked his hand on a thorn.

He woke all the way up. He sat up and looked around. White stars dotted the night sky like snowflakes above the mazy black branches of the thornbush. The wind whistled a low, two-note song through the branches.

For some while now, every time he had fallen asleep in his bed, he had woken up in the dreamland. And every time he had fallen asleep in the dreamland, he had woken up in his own bed.

But now, he had fallen asleep in the dreamland—and woken up there, too.

"I can't get home," he whispered.

He imagined living in the dreamland forever. It had been fun when he was friends with the Other Felix and they were both scared of the monsters. But now that he was friends with the monsters, he was scared of the Other Felix, and nothing was any fun at all. He had a sad, empty feeling as his home with his parents seemed farther and farther away. He started crying. At first he just cried a little, but once he had started, it was as if the tears were forcing their way out of him. He cried harder and couldn't stop. He sobbed, shuddered, and gasped for air until, finally, he was all cried out.

The crying left him feeling tired. He listened to the sounds of the night until the black sky turned violet, then blue, and then pink on one side. Dawn was breaking.

A small bird chittered for a while and then suddenly stopped. Footsteps crunched toward the thornbush.

"Felix," said the Other Felix, "I know you're in there. I heard you crying."

Felix strained his eyes but he couldn't see outside the thick bush.

"You can't be on the side of the monsters," said the Other Felix. "That makes you a monster. And I fight monsters."

"What do you want?" asked Felix.

"I don't want you to go back to the real world. I want you to stay here with me."

"I don't want to stay. You're scaring me."

"Come out of there, Felix."

"No."

"You'd better come out. I'm not going to wait around all day."

"No."

"All right, don't say I didn't warn you."

Warn me? thought Felix. *Warn me about what?*

Through the branches, he saw a dark shape coming closer. Was the Other Felix going to try to crawl into the bush?

He heard a *skrik!* And then he heard it again. There was a crackling sound, like someone crumpling a sheet of stiff, dry paper.

Then he smelled smoke. To make Felix come out, the Other Felix had set the bush on fire.

The crackling grew louder and the smell of smoke grew stronger. Orange light flared. The dry bush was burning quickly.

Felix hesitated. If he crawled out, the Other Felix would be able to shoot him with an arrow. If he waited, he would be burned in the fire. He didn't know if he could die in the dreamland, but it was a chance he didn't want to take.

Lying on his belly, he began crawling under the thorns, away from the fire. The dry branches sounded like snapping, tearing fabric. The smoke was dark and thick, making him cough. Thorns scratched his back, but in moments he was out from under the bush. He stood up. The Other Felix was waiting, his bow drawn back.

"Why are you doing this to me?" asked Felix.

"You know."

"No, I don't."

The Other Felix's arms were trembling. Felix was afraid the arrow would pierce his heart at any moment.

"I was happy before you came here. I didn't know any better. But now I do. You get to go have a family and play with kids and I have to live with these stupid monsters."

Felix began to understand. "So when you started feeling sad . . ."

"I lost my power over the monsters. When you leave, there won't be anything to stop them from eating me."

"But I can't stay here," said Felix. "This isn't my home."

Felix wished he could go to sleep and wake up in his own bed. But the Other Felix would shoot if he tried the sleep trick. The Other Felix's face was hard and angry, but his eyes were soft. A tear glistened on one eyelid.

"You don't have to hate the monsters," said Felix. "I'll show you."

The Other Felix's arms were trembling.

"But I'm afraid," he whispered.

Suddenly, the bow snapped straight. The arrow flew toward Felix. The Other Felix looked surprised.

Felix looked down. He expected to see the fletchings sticking out of his chest. But they weren't there. He turned. The arrow had flown through the burning bush and buried itself in a tree on the other side. It had missed him.

But now the arrow was burning. The tree began burning, too.

"I'm sorry," said the Other Felix.

"I know," said Felix.

"I didn't really want to hurt you. I just never had a friend."

"Me neither."

Behind Felix, the tree burned like a match head, popping and spitting sparks. The sparks fled from tree to tree and soon half the forest was in flames. It burned like the brightest dawn there ever was. All around him, Felix could hear the sounds of frightened monsters fleeing the roaring inferno. He hoped they could run fast enough.

"You'd better go," said the Other Felix.

"I'll miss you," said Felix.

"I'll miss you, too."

The Other Felix lowered his bow. He turned and began running away from the fire with long, loping strides. Felix was glad that the Other Felix would not be burned. But he felt sad for his friend, who would have to live in the dreamland forever, alone.

Suddenly, Felix had a question.

"Do you get older?" he shouted.

The Other Felix stopped and turned.

"I don't know," he answered sadly. And then he ran on, ahead of the raging forest fire.

Suddenly, Felix felt as tired as he had ever felt in his life. Despite the flames and the danger, despite the ovenlike heat from the fire, he was falling asleep. Lying down on the forest floor, he faced up to the flames and closed his eyes.

When he opened them, there was bright sunlight streaming through his bedroom window onto his face. His mother was calling him to wake up.

TWENTY-THREE

After school, Miss Olu asked Felix and Chase to stay behind. Smiling, she told them that she needed their help with a special project. She waited until all the other kids had gone and then closed the door to the classroom.

"I am worried about you, Chase and Felix," she said. "I know that you are both good boys, but you have made bad decisions recently. Felix, you made a bad decision when you took the calculator without permission. Chase, you made a very bad decision when you put my phone in your desk."

Felix wasn't able to look Miss Olu in the eye, so he looked down at the top of his desk instead. He snuck a look out of the corner of his eye and saw that Chase was looking down, too.

"At first I was worried that perhaps you were a bad influence on each other. But I have seen that you do not look at or talk to each other. You are not friends. So probably you are not a bad influence on each other. But maybe you are a bad influence on the other children."

"They say I steal stuff," said Felix miserably.

"And are you innocent? Look me in the eye and tell me you are innocent," said Miss Olu.

Felix couldn't look her in the eye. He hadn't stolen the calculator, but he had taken the phone. And that was much worse.

"Chase? Are you innocent?"

Chase couldn't look Miss Olu in the eye, either.

"If you steal, then you will be called a thief. But I am not worried that either of you will do this again. And, in time, the children will forget what you have done. No, I am much more worried about something else. You are a bad influence because you are unfriendly. I am a friendly woman, and I try to set a good example for you. Most of the children in the class are very friendly. But here you sit, day after day, being very unfriendly to each other."

"What do you want us to do?" asked Felix.

153

"I cannot make you be friends," said Miss Olu. "But I can ask that you speak to each other and show each other respect. And so you will stay after school together one night each week until that is so. I spoke to each of your parents this morning and they gave their permission."

Miss Olu unfolded a piece of paper and gave it to Felix. "Here is a list of the work that I expect you to complete. I will be in the hall, speaking to my beloved family on my phone. It is getting very near their bedtime and they will be expecting my call."

Miss Olu walked out the door, leaving it open behind her. In a moment they heard her musical voice, speaking the language they couldn't understand. She laughed heartily.

Felix and Chase looked at each other.

Chase shrugged. "What does it say?" he asked.

Felix looked at the list. They were to wipe down the whiteboards, empty the pencil sharpeners, take the wastepaper to the recycling bin, water the plants, and close the window shades.

"It's a lot of work," he said.

"Just tell me what it is," said Chase.

Felix told him and said, "I think we should do it in order."

Chase didn't say anything. Felix went to the

whiteboard and picked up an eraser. He climbed on Miss Olu's chair so he could reach the writing at the very top of the board. The floor was a long way down. He was glad he hadn't loosened the screws in the chair. Balancing carefully, he started cleaning the whiteboard. After a minute, Chase came over and picked up another eraser.

They worked without talking. Felix worked slowly and carefully. Chase worked fast and missed a few spots. Felix erased the missed spots when Chase wasn't looking. When they were done, they stacked the erasers in the tray and looked at the list again.

There were two pencil sharpeners. Emptying them took only a minute. Then they picked up the two wastepaper bins and carried them into the hall. Miss Olu was still talking on the phone. She watched them as they carried the bins all the way down the hall and opened the door to the janitor's closet. Felix had seen Mr. Lee going in and out but had never been inside it. He and Chase both stood there for a moment, looking at the shelves stacked with green-wrapped rolls of toilet paper, pink bottles of soap, and white mop heads. The closet smelled clean and musty at the same time.

There was a big blue bin for the paper to be recycled. Chase opened the lid and emptied his bin, and then held the lid open while Felix emptied his. Then Felix took the watering can off a hook next to the big sink and held it under the faucet. Chase turned the cold water handle on and then turned it off when the watering can was full. They walked back down the hall. Felix tried to hold the heavy can steady but some water sloshed out onto his shoes anyway.

Miss Olu's eyes followed them. Felix wanted to make her happy. He decided to say something to Chase, just to show her that he was trying.

"Halfway done," he said.

Chase mumbled a reply.

They went into the room.

"What did you say?" asked Felix.

"I said, this is stupid," said Chase.

Felix didn't know how to answer.

"Give me that," said Chase, reaching for the watering can.

Felix gave Chase the watering can. He watched as Chase went from plant to plant. Chase gave some plants a lot of water and some of them only a little but Felix didn't say anything about it.

Instead he said: "I saw you and your dad yesterday morning."

Chase didn't say anything.

"You know, when the crossing guard got mad at your dad for letting you out in front of school."

"I know," said Chase. "I was there."

"Sorry," said Felix. He wished he hadn't said anything. Chase probably didn't want to be reminded of it.

"My dad's really busy," said Chase. "And my mom's sick. He gets stressed out."

"Yeah, my dad's really busy, too," said Felix. "He's definitely stressed out."

He wasn't actually sure if his father was stressed out, but now that he'd said it, he guessed it was probably true. His father had been working so hard on the Project and things weren't going very well. But at least his father didn't yell at him.

The watering can was empty. Chase put it down on the windowsill.

"What's next?" he asked.

Felix looked at the list. "Why do you think monsters are stupid?"

"What?"

"The first day you came to school, you said that monsters are stupid."

Chase looked over Felix's head, trying to remember. "I did?"

Felix nodded.

"They're not always stupid. Sometimes they're cool."

"It depends on the monster," agreed Felix.

To close the window shades, the boys had to climb on top of the radiator covers, something they were not allowed to do during class. They looked at the radiator covers, then at each other. Chase smiled a little bit. Felix knew what he was thinking. He smiled a little bit, too. Felix went to one end of the long row of windows and Chase went to the other end. They climbed onto the radiator covers and stood up. One by one, they began pulling the shades closed, working their way toward each other in the middle of the room.

TWENTY-FOUR

"Felix, where are you?" asked his mother at dinner that night. Felix was lost in thought. He had hardly noticed that his mother had made his favorite dinner, cheese-and-potato pierogies, or that his father had come home early. His parents had been talking about something that seemed important, but Felix hadn't heard a word of it. He was thinking about bedtime.

Felix's mother asked him where he was two more times that evening. The first time, she was helping him with his homework and it was as if someone had turned down the volume on her voice. Her lips moved but Felix didn't hear anything.

The second time was while he was reading to her. He was staring at the words on the page and thought he had been reading them aloud. But after his mother waved her hand in front of his face to get his attention, she told him that he hadn't said anything for a minute.

Gently, she took the book from his hands and closed it. "Felix, are you all right?"

"I'm worried," he told her.

"Are you worried about what your father and I were talking about at dinner?"

Felix shook his head.

"Good," she said. "Because everything's going to be fine."

"I'm wondering what's going to happen tonight when I fall asleep."

"When you fall asleep? Well, you'll fall asleep, your body will rest, and you'll dream."

"That's what I'm afraid of," said Felix.

"Dreaming is good," said his mother. "Even when dreams are confusing to us, they help our brains make sense of everything that's happening in our lives."

And after an extra-long back rub and a song— even though he asked her not to, Felix's mother sang "Over the Rainbow"—he fell asleep.

TWENTY-FIVE

He did dream that night. And, in his dream, he
saw the dreamland, as he always did. But this
time, he wasn't in the dreamland—he was only
watching it. It was as though he were floating or
flying, and every time he blinked, he found himself
somewhere new.

He saw the clearing in the forest where he'd
first entered the dreamland. He saw the stone steps
and the field of boulders. He saw the raft on the
riverbank, tethered to a tree. He saw the burned
forest in the hidden valley. He saw the broad green
valley and the wooden tower. All the rooms in the
tower were empty. The Other Felix's bow and arrows were hanging on their pegs.

Then he saw a trail. The Other Felix was climbing. His eyes sparkled and his expression was determined.

The Other Felix kept going until he reached the pools. Without stopping, he climbed past the pools to the cleft in the rock where the monsters lived. He disappeared into the cleft.

Then Felix was inside, too, watching.

The Other Felix climbed up the trail until monsters' caves were all around. Then he stopped and took off his backpack. He cupped his hands around his mouth and shouted.

"Monsters! Come out!"

There was no sound.

"Monsters! It's me, Felix!" called the Other Felix.

Now the monsters answered, in high-pitched shrieks and low rumbles, in snorts and grunts and wet slurps that sounded like the licking of lips.

The Other Felix opened his backpack. "I brought sandwiches and cookies," he said.

The monsters came rushing out of their caves. There were so many of them, and they came so quickly, that it looked as though they would crush the Other Felix. But they didn't. In moments, the huge creatures were arranged in an obedient circle around the small boy, who went from beak to snout to gaping maw, feeding them sandwiches.

When a monster that looked like an aardvark crossed with an ostrich started snuffling in the backpack, the Other Felix gave it a gentle shove.

"You can't have a cookie until you've eaten your sandwich," he said with a smile.

Sulking, the monster sat back down in the dirt and waited for its sandwich.

After all the sandwiches and cookies were gone, the monsters waited, watching the Other Felix expectantly. They were so big, and the sandwiches had been so small, that Felix was sure they were still hungry. But the Other Felix didn't seem the least bit worried.

"Now," he said, "we're going to play tag."

And that is exactly what they did. How the Other Felix kept from being crushed was a mystery, but he ran fearlessly among the monsters, darting under their bodies, leaping over their tails, dodging around their thudding legs. Once or twice he was sent sprawling by a monster's tag, but each time, he picked himself up, slapped the dust from his clothes, and chased the nearest monster until he could deliver a well-timed swat and shout, "You're it!"

The whole thing was so funny that Felix would have laughed, if he weren't dreaming. But soon the Other Felix, filthy and sweating, was laughing. Even the monsters began laughing, a sound so funny that it made the Other Felix laugh even harder. Because a monster laughing sounds like an elephant coughing up a hair ball.

As the dust rose under the players' feet, Felix began rising, too. He rose higher and higher in the air and the monsters grew smaller and smaller. The Other Felix became a dot, then a speck, then disappeared into the cloud of dust.

TWENTY-SIX

After school, Felix was walking down the hall toward the stairs when he saw his father standing outside the principal's office. His father was frowning at the crowd of kids rushing past him. He almost looked as if he were lost. But when he saw Felix, he smiled and waved.

Felix looked at Chase, who happened to be walking beside him. Chase shrugged. He didn't know what this unplanned visit meant, either. Felix went over to his father.

"Hi," he said.

Felix's father rubbed the top of Felix's head. "I thought I'd get you today. Is that all right?"

Felix nodded. He followed his father down the

stairs and out the door. They stopped on the side-walk in front of the school. Felix's father looked very serious. Felix didn't know what was happening. His father had never picked him up from school before.

"I have to tell you something, Felix," said his father. "The Project failed. We all worked as hard as we could, and we tried everything we could think of doing, but it didn't work out. We didn't get the money we needed and so the whole thing's over. All that work, and now I'm out of a job."

Felix's father's mouth made a small smile, but his eyes were sad. His voice sounded shaky. Felix had never seen his father like this.

"Does it mean I can't go to school anymore?" asked Felix. "Will we have to move to another city where we don't know anybody and I'll be the new kid in class? Will we be poor?"

Felix's father made a funny sound. It sounded kind of like coughing and kind of like laughing, too. He cleared his throat. Shaking his head, he wiped his eyes with the back of his hand. Then he laughed some more.

"No," said his father. "No, those things won't happen. At least I don't think so, and if they do, they won't happen for a long time."

Felix was confused. "Then why are you picking me up from school?"

His father stopped laughing. "Because I wanted to see you. I thought we could go to the zoo."

"What about Mrs. Nowak?"

"Do you want her to come, too?"

"No, I—"

"I'm only teasing, Felix. I've already told her you're going to be with me."

They rode the bus to the zoo. There was hardly anyone there. It was late afternoon on a school day, after all, and the weather wasn't very nice. The sky was gray and the air was crisp and wintry. As they walked, their fingers and noses and ears grew red and cold. But they didn't mind. They drank hot chocolate and ate buttery popcorn and a big pretzel with salt and mustard. Felix's father bought him a balloon, and even though Felix was too old for balloons, he let his father tie the string around his wrist and pretended that he was excited about it. The wind kept wrapping the balloon around them and at first it was annoying but then after a while it made them both laugh until they had tears coming out of their eyes.

They saw everything: mammals, birds, fish, reptiles, and bugs. They took off their jackets in the steamy African Journey exhibit and zipped them up again as they shivered in the penguin house. They looked for animals in the forest at the Children's Zoo but they didn't see any.

They spent most of their time looking at the biggest animals. At a bear who paced around the edges of his rocky enclosure. At the lions who lay in a heap on some hay, their tails twitching as they dreamed. And at the elephants, whose wise eyes peered peacefully out of their pebbly hides.

When he was small, Felix had been afraid of these animals. Once, after a lion roared, he had begged his parents to take him home. He had heard the lion's roar in other sounds—in revving car engines and descending jet planes—for weeks. It had been so easy to imagine the lion leaping across the pit to where he stood watching. And surely the gorillas could have broken the glass with their big, strong hands? But now he wasn't afraid of them. Now he wondered whether the animals missed the forests that had been their homes, whether they wondered fearfully about this strange new place in which they found themselves. And whether the lions, when they dreamed, went somewhere far away, where they were happy.

Felix's father had grown quiet. Felix looked up. His father was staring into the lions' enclosure as if it were empty. His hands were hanging by his sides. Felix grabbed his father's hand and squeezed.

"Don't be scared, Dad," he said. "Everything will be okay." He paused. "If I can learn to fight monsters, then you can get another job."

His father squeezed back. "You know how to fight monsters?" he asked.

Felix nodded. "It's not as hard as it sounds. And I can show you how to do it, too."